Sutradhaar

by

Bhirgu Shukla

"Where words failed, the thread spoke"

25th July 2025

PREFACE

"Sutradhaar – The Invisible Thread of Love"

Some stories are not written with ink.
They are sewn gently into the fabric of time,
With emotions, silences, glances, and the ache of two hearts waiting to be understood.

This is not a love story born in chaos or rebellion.
Yeh kahani hai un do logon ki jo milte toh ek rasmein nibhaane ke liye hain,
par bichhad jaate toh zindagi adhoori reh jaati.

Sutradhaar is the tale of a thread,
An invisible *dor* spun by fate, pulled softly by emotion,
and held tightly by two souls who never planned to fall in love,
but did,slowly, deeply, irrevocably.

The characters you will meet in these pages are not just protagonists of a plot.
They are whispers of your own heart.
A boy who didn't expect to find poetry in her silence.
A girl who feared losing herself,but found herself in his love.
A bond born not in fire, but in trust, warmth, and time.

As the story unfolds, you'll find pieces of yourself in their hesitation,
their laughter, their longing, and their surrender.

I've named it "**Sutradhaar**" for a reason.

In classical Sanskrit drama, the *Sutradhaar* is the narrator,the one who connects each scene, each emotion, each twist of fate.
In this novel, love itself plays that role.
It connects two strangers not just through a marriage,
but through layered conversations, emotional undressing, and silent companionship.
Jahan lafzon se zyada ahsaas bolte hain.
Jahan ek nazar, ek raat, ek chhoti si baat,kisi ki poori duniya badal deti hai.

This story is personal, because it reminds us that love doesn't always knock with grand gestures.
Kabhi kabhi, woh ek doorbell hoti hai, ek chai ki chuski hoti hai, ek shared cab ride hoti hai,
ya ek shaadi ka rishta,jo dil ke raaste se guzarta hai.

It is for the lovers who met late, but loved right.
For the girls who feared love would steal their freedom.
For the boys who dared to love with softness, not pride.

May *Sutradhaar* remind you that some threads aren't meant to be seen,
They are meant to be felt.
And once tied, they never loosen.

Bhirgu Shukla

(With love, from the thread between two souls to the hearts that will read this story)

Who am I?

I, Me, and Myself, three different souls that live inside Bhirgu Shukla. They are not metaphors. They are real, distinct, and often at war. Bhirgu himself doesn't exist as a singular emotion or identity, he is the space between them. He is incomplete without the voices that speak through him: the silent one, the broken one, the hopeful one. You won't find him in a crowd, nor will he demand to be heard, but you will find his truth scattered in words, like dust across a forgotten road.

Bhirgu is, by his own admission, **anhedonic** , he finds no joy in the usual pleasures of the world. He doesn't chase validation or seek comfort in people's approval. He does not write to impress. He writes because something inside him refuses to stay silent. In a world where everyone is trying to feel more, Bhirgu has learned to survive by feeling less, and in that paradox lies his strength.

This novel was not written in celebration, but in survival. **Sutradhaar** was born from the third voice, the invisible observer. The man who watches love, loses love, and still chooses to honor it. This book is not a tale of victory or romance; it is a meditation on what it means to **love without expectation**, to remain loyal to someone in spirit long after they've left in body. It is about choosing a place within your heart to keep them, not because you won, but because they mattered.

Bhirgu doesn't believe stories are just stories, he believes they are confessions. This novel is his. It reflects the inner life of a man torn between the simplicity of his village and the exhaustion of the city, between ambition and peace, between being seen and being understood. It tells the story of a man who never stops trying, even when he knows things won't go right. Because sometimes, the most courageous thing is to live in the wrong and still try to make something beautiful out of it.

He writes not because he feels everything, but because he feels **something**. And that something, however small, is enough to carry a story.

"वो लौटे भी तो कहाँ लौटे,
जो चले थे दलि में उतरने...
अब दलि ही उजड़ा पड़ा है कहीं,
और रास्‌ते भी थक चुके हैं।"

-Gulzar

Chapter 1

The First Step into Silence

"जो बीत गई सो बात गई।"

-Harivansh Rai Bachchan

(What has passed is gone, let us not cling, but move forward.)

The scent of woodsmoke and damp earth clung to Kumar like a second skin, a familiar perfume that would soon be replaced by the sharp, unfamiliar tang of Delhi. His village, nestled in the heart of Uttar Pradesh, was a tapestry woven from emerald paddy fields, terracotta rooftops, and the rhythmic chirping of crickets. It was a life he knew intimately, a life etched in the lines of his father's weathered face, the warmth of his mother's embrace, and the playful banter of his siblings. His father, a respected priest, his life a quiet devotion to the village temple and its people, had instilled in Kumar a deep-seated respect for tradition and community. Life was simple, predictable, sometimes harsh, but always comforting in its familiarity. Yet, a restless energy pulsed beneath the surface of Kumar's quiet demeanor, a yearning for something more, something beyond the horizon of his familiar world.

The village school, with its worn desks and chalk-dusted blackboards, had only offered a glimpse of the vast expanse of knowledge that lay beyond. Books, dog-eared and precious, became his escape, their pages filled with tales of bustling cities and ambitious dreams. Delhi, a distant, shimmering mirage, represented a world of opportunity, a chance to break free from the cyclical rhythms of village life and carve his own path. He dreamt of universities, of libraries filled with untold stories, of a life where his potential wouldn't be constrained by the limitations of his small village.

The decision to leave hadn't been easy. The weight of his family's expectations, the unspoken worry etched in his mother's eyes, the silent pride in his father's gaze, these were anchors to his heart. He knew his departure would leave a void, a silence in the familiar melody of their lives. The farewells were a symphony of bittersweet emotions. His father's quiet blessing, a hand resting on Kumar’s shoulder, spoke volumes of unspoken hopes and fears. His mother's tearful embrace, a silent prayer for his safety and success, tightened his throat with an ache that words couldn't express. His siblings, their faces a mixture of envy and admiration, promised to keep the home fires burning until his return.

The journey to Delhi was a blur of dusty roads, crowded buses, and the constant hum of anticipation. As the familiar landscape gave way to the sprawling urban sprawl, a mixture of excitement and trepidation took root in Kumar's heart. He clutched the worn leather bag containing his meagre belongings – a few sets of clothes, his cherished books, and the blessings of his family. He was a young man venturing into the unknown, armed with only his determination, his dreams, and the unwavering support of his loved ones. The city loomed before him, a concrete jungle promising both adventure and challenges.

The old Rajendra Nagar area welcomed him with a cacophony of sounds – the relentless honking of vehicles, the boisterous chatter of vendors, the rhythmic clang of metal against metal from nearby workshops. The air hung heavy with the aroma of street food, a mixture of tantalizing spices and the pervasive scent of exhaust fumes. The narrow lanes, teeming with people, presented a stark contrast to the quiet serenity of his village. The sheer density of the population was overwhelming, a stark shift from the open spaces and tranquil rhythms of his rural upbringing.

Finding his paying guest accommodation was an ordeal in itself. The PG, a cramped space with shared bathrooms and a perpetually buzzing atmosphere, was a far cry from the comfort of his family home. Navigating the city's labyrinthine streets, deciphering the cryptic routes of the public transport system, and managing his meagre finances proved to be a daily struggle. His initial naiveté and vulnerability were palpable, and the city, initially a beacon of hope, occasionally felt like a hostile and unforgiving entity. He missed the familiar faces, the comforting routines, the simplicity of his village life. The initial weeks were a blur of hurried mornings, crammed classes, and long, exhausting evenings. He juggled his studies with part-time jobs – tutoring younger students, assisting at a small shop, even delivering newspapers before dawn. Each rupee earned was a victory, a testament to his unwavering determination to make a life for himself in this demanding city. He sent money home whenever possible, a small token of his gratitude and a promise of a better future for his family. His dreams and ambitions remained his guiding stars, a beacon of light in the often-overwhelming darkness of his new reality. The city, despite its challenges, was starting to feel like a place where his potential could flourish. He was adapting, learning, and slowly finding his place in this bustling metropolis. The transition wasn't easy, but his spirit remained unbroken. His resolve to succeed, to build a brighter future for himself and his family, was his constant companion. His longing for home was always present, a quiet ache in his heart. Yet, he embraced the challenges and the excitement that Delhi had to offer.

His days were a whirlwind of activity, a mix of academic pursuit, financial struggles, and a growing sense of belonging. Each experience was a new layer in the ever-evolving tapestry of his urban life, a vibrant contrast to the gentle tranquility of his village past.

The rickshaw lurched violently, throwing Kumar against the worn, vinyl seat. The driver, a wiry man with eyes that seemed to hold the secrets of a thousand Delhi nights, weaved expertly through the chaotic traffic, a human chess piece navigating a game of impossible odds. Horns blared, a cacophony of metallic screams that assaulted Kumar's ears, a sound completely alien to the quiet, rural landscape he had left behind. The air, thick with the aroma of exhaust fumes and street food, hung heavy in his lungs, a pungent cocktail that was both intoxicating and suffocating.
Old Rajendra Nagar unfolded before him like a vibrant, chaotic tapestry. Narrow lanes, barely wide enough for two rickshaws to pass, teemed with people – a swirling vortex of humanity. Vendors hawked their wares, their voices a rhythmic chant rising above the din of the city. The scent of spices – cardamom, cloves, cumin – mingled with the metallic tang of freshly-cut metal from the nearby workshops, creating a sensory overload that both thrilled and overwhelmed Kumar. He watched, mesmerized and slightly terrified, as motorbikes zipped past, narrowly avoiding collisions, their riders a blur of motion. The contrast to the peaceful serenity of his village was stark, almost jarring. The quiet rhythm of his rural life, punctuated by the gentle sounds of nature, was replaced by a relentless, frenetic energy that pulsed through the very veins of the city.

His paying guest accommodation was a far cry from the comfort and familiarity of his family home. A cramped room in a shared building, the walls thin enough to hear the hushed conversations and occasional arguments of his neighbours, it felt less like a home and more like a temporary holding cell in the vast urban prison. The shared bathroom, perpetually damp and smelling faintly of mildew, was a source of constant frustration. The kitchen, a small, cluttered space, was dominated by the relentless hum of a worn-out refrigerator and the clatter of utensils. Yet, despite its limitations, it was shelter, a refuge in the bewildering sprawl of the city.

Navigating the city's labyrinthine streets was an adventure in itself. The bus routes, a cryptic collection of numbers and abbreviations, were a source of constant confusion. He often found himself lost, wandering aimlessly through crowded markets, the faces of strangers a blur, the sounds a deafening roar. He missed the familiar landmarks of his village, the comforting predictability of its routines. Here, in Delhi, everything was uncertain, everything was a challenge. The simple act of crossing the road was a perilous undertaking, a daring feat of agility and survival.

Managing his finances was a constant struggle. The meagre allowance his father had managed to scrape together felt like grains of sand slipping through his fingers. Every rupee was precious, each expense meticulously accounted for in a small notebook, a tangible record of his financial precariousness. The cost of food, accommodation, and transport, even the occasional cup of chai, gnawed at his savings. He supplemented his allowance by taking on part-time jobs, tutoring younger students in mathematics and Hindi, a skill he had honed during his village years. The work was demanding, tiring, but essential, every extra rupee a small victory against the overwhelming odds.

His initial vulnerability and naiveté were painfully apparent. He fell prey to petty scams, his inexperience easily exploited. The city, initially a beacon of hope, occasionally felt like a hostile, unforgiving entity. The loneliness was a heavy cloak, weighing down on his spirits. He missed the familiar faces, the comforting routines, the simple joys of his village life. He missed his family, their unwavering support, their silent prayers. Their love was a constant source of strength, a reminder of the life he had left behind, a hope for the future he was striving to build.

Yet, amidst the challenges and uncertainties, a small spark of resilience ignited within him. He saw the city not as a cruel mistress, but as a challenging lover, demanding commitment, hard work and a relentless pursuit of his goals. The faces of his fellow students, many of them battling their own struggles, instilled in him a sense of camaraderie. He found solace in the shared experience of their hardships and the mutual support they offered one another.

The city was a harsh teacher, but a teacher nonetheless. He learnt to haggle with vendors, to navigate the crowded buses with practiced ease, to spot the scams and to avoid them. He learned the unspoken rules of urban survival, the art of blending into the anonymous chaos of the city. He discovered hidden pockets of beauty and tranquility within the city's urban sprawl. He found solace in the quiet corners of libraries, immersing himself in the world of literature. He discovered hidden gems - little cafes, tucked away on quiet side streets, where he could savour a cup of chai and watch the city life unfold around him.

The early mornings, once a blur of hurried preparation, became structured moments of quiet reflection, a time for introspection and planning before the day's relentless demands. His nights, often spent poring over his textbooks, were punctuated by the sounds of the city – a constant reminder that he was still a stranger in a strange land. He embraced this reality, finding strength in his own adaptability and determination.

Evenings often brought relief, a time to relax and reflect. He would wander the streets, observing the rhythm of the city, the intricate dance of people navigating their lives within this vibrant, pulsating heart of India. The city was teaching him patience, resilience, and the importance of adapting to unforeseen challenges, a crucial lesson in his journey to build a life away from the comforting predictability of his rural past. He began to see the city not as a source of fear or loneliness, but as an opportunity, a canvas on which he could paint his own destiny. His days were still demanding, filled with academic rigour, financial struggles, and the constant need to adjust. However, the intensity of his experiences helped him grow stronger, more adaptable, and more determined than ever before. Every challenge, every obstacle, was a stepping stone on his path to success, a path paved with resilience and a thirst for achieving his dreams. The constant hum of the city's energy became the backdrop of his life, a constant reminder of the vastness of possibilities that unfolded before him, a challenge he was not merely ready to accept, but to embrace.

The aroma of freshly brewed chai, sharp and invigorating, cut through the humid Delhi air. Kumar, clutching his worn textbook, hesitated at the entrance of a small eatery, its bright yellow paint chipped and faded, but its air buzzing

with a lively energy. He'd been studying relentlessly, fueled by lukewarm tea and stale biscuits, and the hunger gnawing at his stomach finally overpowered his frugality. Inside, the air was thick with the scent of spices and frying onions, a comforting counterpoint to the sterile environment of his cramped PG room.

He found a seat on a wobbly plastic chair, the thin metal digging into his thighs, and ordered a plate of steaming aloo paratha and a cup of chai. As he ate, his eyes scanned the room, taking in the diverse tapestry of Delhi life unfolding around him. Students hunched over textbooks, their faces illuminated by the soft glow of flickering fluorescent lights. Office workers, their ties loosened, engaged in animated conversations over their meals. A family, their laughter echoing through the room, shared a single plate of biryani. The space felt like a microcosm of the city itself – chaotic, vibrant, and full of unspoken stories.

It was then he saw her. She sat at a table near the window, bathed in the warm afternoon light. Her dark hair, pulled back in a neat ponytail, framed a face both intelligent and strikingly beautiful. She wore a simple cotton salwar kameez, but her demeanor radiated an aura of quiet confidence, a stark contrast to his own hesitant awkwardness. She was engrossed in a thick textbook, a determined furrow in her brow, occasionally pausing to make notes in a well-worn notebook. Even from a distance, her focus, her intensity, was captivating.

He found himself watching her, mesmerized, stealing glances whenever he could. She seemed oblivious to his gaze, completely immersed in her studies. The intensity with which she approached her work was admirable. There was a quiet strength about her that resonated deeply with him, a quality he both admired and felt slightly intimidated by. He wondered what she was studying, what dreams fueled her relentless dedication.

He finished his meal, a sense of unease settling in his stomach. He wanted to speak to her, to somehow break the invisible barrier that separated them, but the thought filled him with a crippling shyness. He'd always been a shy boy, even in his village, but in the anonymity of the city, his reticence felt magnified, almost suffocating.

Just as he was about to leave, defeated by his own apprehension, she looked up, her eyes meeting his across the crowded room. There was a flicker of surprise in her gaze, followed by a small, almost imperceptible smile. He felt his cheeks flush, a wave of heat spreading through his body. The simple act of her acknowledgement, the briefest of connections, felt like a lifeline thrown into a sea of uncertainty.

Gathering his courage, he cleared his throat, a sound that seemed ridiculously loud in the sudden silence. He approached her table, his heart hammering against his ribs, a frantic drumbeat echoing in his ears. "Excuse me," he began, his voice barely a whisper, "Is this seat taken?" He gestured to the empty chair opposite her.

She looked at the chair, then back at him, her gaze lingering for a moment longer than necessary. "No," she replied, her voice clear and melodious, "it's free." There was a warmth in her tone that eased his nervousness, a hint of something else he couldn't quite decipher.

He sat down, the plastic chair creaking under his weight. An awkward silence hung between them, broken only by the low hum of conversation and the clatter of cutlery. He fumbled with his textbook, avoiding her gaze, unsure of what to say.

Finally, he mumbled, "I… I'm Kumar. Kumar Tiwari.

She smiled again, a genuine, radiant smile that lit up her face. "Chitra," she said, extending her hand. He took it, her touch surprisingly firm and confident. Her hand felt warm, sending a surprising jolt through him.

"*Chitra Sharma*," she added, as if sensing his slight hesitation. "I'm preparing for the UPSC exams."

He nodded, impressed. "Oh," he replied, "That's… that's amazing." He felt a surge of admiration for her ambition, a quality he both envied and respected. He knew nothing of her world, of the rigorous preparation she was undertaking, yet he felt a strange connection to her relentless pursuit of her goals. It echoed his own journey, his own struggle to find his place in this unforgiving city. They talked for what felt like hours, the initial awkwardness melting away with each passing moment. He learned that she lived in a nearby neighbourhood, that she'd been studying tirelessly for years, her dreams as ambitious as they were demanding. He told her about his village, about his family, about his studies, painting a picture of his simple life, a world so different from hers, yet somehow strangely familiar.

He discovered that she appreciated his quiet nature, his simple honesty, finding a refreshing contrast in his unassuming manner to the often-superficial interactions of city life. There was an ease in their conversation, a comfortable rhythm that surprised both of them. Their different backgrounds, their contrasting lifestyles, seemed to melt away, replaced by a shared understanding of the struggles and aspirations that united them, both driven by a burning desire to create a better future for themselves.

As the afternoon light faded, casting long shadows across the eatery, they exchanged numbers, a silent promise hanging in the air. The initial contact, a chance encounter in a crowded eatery, felt like the start of something extraordinary, a connection that transcended the chaotic backdrop of their lives, a spark of hope amid the complexities of the city. He walked home that evening, his heart lighter than it had been in weeks, a new rhythm setting in, a counterpoint to the city's relentless beat. The city, once a place of daunting challenges, felt slightly less hostile, a little more welcoming, thanks to a chance encounter with a girl named Chitra. The aroma of chai, once a simple comfort, now held a new, sweet fragrance, tinged with the promise of something beautiful to come. The future remained uncertain, but for the first time since his arrival in Delhi, Kumar felt a glimmer of optimism, a fragile hope taking root in the concrete jungle.

The days that followed were a whirlwind of stolen moments and quiet gestures. Kumar found himself drawn to Chitra's world, a world of meticulously organized notes, late-night study sessions fueled by strong coffee, and the relentless pressure of the UPSC exams. He watched her, captivated by her dedication, her unwavering focus, her quiet determination. He'd never encountered such single-minded pursuit of a goal, and it both intimidated and inspired him. He found himself wanting to be a part of it, to contribute in some small way to her success. Initially, his help was small, almost insignificant. He'd offer to carry her heavy textbooks, his arms aching under the weight, a silent act of service. He'd fetch her chai from the little eatery where they first met, the aroma now inextricably linked to the memory of their first conversation. He'd offer to run errands, picking up stationery or snacks, his willingness born of a deep-seated desire to be near her.

As he spent more time with Chitra, he saw a vulnerability beneath her composed exterior, a quiet anxiety that bubbled beneath the surface of her focused energy. The pressure of the exams, the weight of expectations, weighed heavily on her. He noticed the late nights, the tired eyes, the occasional moments of self-doubt that flickered across her face. He wanted to ease her burden, to offer a respite from the relentless pressure.

His devotion to Chitra wasn't merely romantic; it was rooted in a profound admiration for her strength and her unyielding spirit. He saw in her a reflection of his own aspirations – a longing for a better future, a desire to transcend the limitations of his past. Her ambition, her resilience, resonated deeply within him, fueling his own determination to support her in any way he could.

His own financial situation was precarious. He was struggling to make ends meet, juggling his studies with part-time jobs, often working late into the night, his exhaustion a constant companion. Yet, he never hesitated to sacrifice his own comfort for Chitra's needs. He took on extra shifts, foregoing sleep and personal time, his efforts fueled by a quiet love that demanded nothing in return. He felt a deep sense of fulfillment in supporting her, in contributing to her success, seeing his efforts reflected in the gleam of hope in her eyes.

One evening, as Chitra was hunched over a mountain of textbooks, her face etched with exhaustion, Kumar noticed a small tear trace a path down her cheek. He saw her struggle, her self-doubt creeping in, and his heart ached for her. He gently touched her arm, his touch hesitant, unsure.

“Chitra,” he whispered, his voice soft and reassuring, “You’re doing amazing. You’re so close.”

She looked up, her eyes red-rimmed, her expression a mixture of exhaustion and gratitude. “It’s just… so much pressure,” she admitted, her voice trembling slightly. “I’m not sure I can do it.”

Kumar’s heart sank. He knew how much this meant to her, how much she'd poured into her studies. He reached out and gently took her hand, his touch conveying a silent promise of support.

“You can,” he said, his voice firm and unwavering. “I know you can. I’ll be here for you, every step of the way.”

His words were simple, but they carried the weight of his unwavering devotion. He wasn’t just offering words of encouragement; he was offering his unwavering support, his steadfast presence, a constant reminder that she wasn't alone in her struggle.

His actions spoke louder than words. He started helping her with her studies, patiently explaining concepts she found challenging, his own knowledge proving unexpectedly useful. He meticulously organized her notes, creating a system that helped her navigate the vast sea of information. He'd quiz her on topics, gently correcting her mistakes, his guidance a blend of support and encouragement.

He discovered a quiet joy in these small acts of service. He found fulfillment in supporting her, in witnessing her growth and progress. He understood the nuances of her ambitions, her dreams, and her fears. He didn't just see her as a brilliant scholar; he saw her as a complex, beautiful, vulnerable woman, and his love for her deepened with each shared moment of struggle and triumph.

He started bringing her small gifts, little tokens of his affection – a single flower from the roadside vendor, a packet of her favorite biscuits, a handwritten note expressing his admiration for her strength and determination. These simple gestures, born from a genuine love for her, spoke volumes about the depth of his feelings.

His devotion extended beyond the realm of academics. He noticed that she often skipped meals, too engrossed in her studies to take a break. He started packing her lunches, ensuring she had nutritious food to sustain her through long study sessions. He would wait for her outside the library, his presence a comforting constant in her demanding schedule. His care extended beyond the purely academic, encompassing her physical and emotional well-being.

He began to understand the subtle rhythm of her life, her needs, her struggles. He learned to anticipate her requirements, offering support before she even had to ask. His love for her wasn't a grand, sweeping gesture; it was a quiet, steady current that flowed beneath the surface of their everyday lives. It was in the small, unassuming acts of kindness, in the quiet gestures of support, that his true devotion revealed itself. His love for Chitra wasn't just about romantic feelings; it was about unwavering support, a commitment to help her achieve her dreams, even at the expense of his own comfort and convenience. It was a devotion that stemmed from a deep admiration, respect, and a profound understanding of the woman he loved.

His sacrifices went largely unnoticed, he never sought recognition or praise. His love was a silent force, a quiet strength that sustained Chitra through the trials and tribulations of her UPSC preparation. He never complained, never faltered, his devotion a constant beacon in the darkness of her rigorous study schedule. He often felt like a silent guardian angel, watching over her, protecting her, and silently celebrating every small victory she achieved. The city, once a symbol of loneliness and anonymity, had transformed into a canvas of their shared journey, a testament to his unwavering devotion and their budding love story. The clatter of the city, once a harsh symphony, now harmonized with the soft rhythm of their shared dreams. The aroma of chai, once simply a pleasant fragrance, now held the sweet scent of shared moments, mutual support, and an enduring love blooming amidst the chaos of urban India. The city, once a daunting obstacle, had now become the stage for their beautiful, quiet romance. His love was a quiet symphony, a silent ode to the woman who had captured his heart and soul, a story unfolding quietly in the bustling heart of Delhi. The city witnessed their unspoken vows, a silent promise of love, support, and a future together, a testament to a devotion that transcended the concrete jungle.

The weight of expectations pressed down on Kumar like the humid Delhi air, clinging to him, heavy and suffocating. It wasn't just the pressure of his own studies; his family back in the village expected so much from him. He was the first to venture into the city, to seek higher education, to break the cycle of subsistence farming that had defined generations of his family. He carried the hopes and dreams of his entire village on his shoulders, a burden he often felt he couldn't bear alone. Each letter from his father, filled with the rustic fragrance of the village and laced with quiet pride, also carried the silent weight of responsibility. His father's words, simple yet profound, echoed in his ears: "Son, this is our chance, our escape. Don't let us down."

The city, initially alluring with its promise of opportunity, was now a relentless crucible, testing his limits in ways he'd never imagined. The academic rigors were formidable, demanding long hours of study, sacrificing sleep and social life. He attended classes, often fueled by lukewarm chai and stale biscuits, the remnants of his meager budget. His part-time job at a small tea stall, barely covered his rent and food expenses, leaving little left for books or stationary. Every rupee was accounted for, meticulously budgeted, each expense a battle fought and won with grit and determination. He yearned for the simpler life of his village, where meals were shared, worries were eased by the comforting rhythm of village life

The loneliness gnawed at him. He missed the familiar faces, the comforting presence of family and friends. The city, vast and anonymous, felt isolating despite the constant human swarm. He often found himself longing for the open fields, the starry nights, the familiar warmth of the village hearth. The city, while promising opportunities, had also brought with it a stark isolation. He missed the comfort of community, the support system that had always been a part of his life back in the village. The transition hadn't been easy. He often found himself wrestling with feelings of homesickness and self-doubt, a bitter contrast to the confident and ambitious persona he presented to the world.

His relationship with Chitra added another layer of complexity to his struggles. He wanted to be the perfect partner, the supportive companion she needed, but the constant pressure of his studies and work made it difficult. He longed to spend more time with her, to share the quiet moments that he cherished, but his schedule was unrelenting. He felt a deep pang of guilt when he couldn't give her the attention he wished he could, his heart aching at the knowledge that he was falling short. He wrestled with the conflict between his desire to succeed academically and his commitment to nurturing their relationship, a tug-of-war between his personal aspirations and his growing affection for Chitra.

He found himself torn between two worlds. The quiet, familiar world of his village, with its predictable rhythms and strong community ties, and the chaotic, demanding world of the city, with its unrelenting pressure and isolating anonymity. He carried the weight of both worlds on his shoulders, a burden that threatened to crush him. Yet, he persisted, driven by a deep-seated desire to succeed, to honor the expectations placed upon him, and to build a life that both he and Chitra could share. The city, once a beacon of hope, was now a battlefield, where he fought not only for his future but for their shared dreams.

The financial constraints weighed heavily on him. The meager earnings from his part-time job felt like drops in a vast ocean of expenses. He often found himself rationing his food, skipping meals to save money, his stomach often gnawing with hunger. He'd walk extra miles to save on bus fare, his feet aching from the long journey, his body protesting the strain. The city's relentless pace was a stark contrast to the slower, more leisurely pace of his village life, and he felt the weight of that change acutely. The constant struggle for survival, even amid his aspirations, was a constant reminder of the harsh realities of city life.

Yet, even in his struggle, his love for Chitra provided a flicker of hope, a beacon in the darkness. He found solace in their shared moments, in the quiet intimacy of their stolen conversations. He would steal moments to walk with her through the bustling markets, to share a cup of chai at a street vendor, the sweet aroma a temporary respite from the harsh realities of city life. Her presence brought comfort, providing a sense of belonging amidst the isolation. It was in these stolen moments that he found the strength to endure, her unwavering faith in him a powerful motivator.

He continued to support Chitra in her UPSC preparations, tirelessly helping her with her studies, even amidst his own academic and financial pressures. He would organize her notes, highlight important passages, and offer words of encouragement when doubt crept in. He'd often stay up late into the night, reviewing her materials, despite his own fatigue. His love for her fueled his commitment to her success, transcending his own personal struggles. His efforts were not about receiving recognition, but about helping someone he deeply cared about to reach her full potential. It was an act of pure devotion, a silent testament to the depth of his feelings.

The city, once a symbol of hope and opportunity, now felt like a constant battleground. But in the midst of it all, Kumar clung to the promise of a better future, for himself and for Chitra. His determination fueled his efforts, his love for Chitra his guiding star, leading him through the dark and turbulent waters of city life. The city tested his resilience, challenged his limits, yet simultaneously forged his spirit. The weight of expectations, both personal and familial, pressed down on him, but it was in the face of this adversity that his true strength emerged, a quiet strength born of love, determination, and an unwavering commitment to his dreams. His journey in the city was a testament to his capacity for resilience, his unwavering belief in a brighter future, and the profound and transforming power of love amidst the overwhelming realities of life in a bustling Indian metropolis.

Chapter 2

In Rooms Without Names

"भीड़ में अकेले चलना भी एक हुनर है, जो हर कसिी के बस की बात नहीं।"

- Rahat Indori

(Walking alone in a crowd is also an art, not everyone can master it.)

The aroma of filter coffee, usually a comforting start to their day, now hung heavy in the air, a stark contrast to the unspoken tension that had settled between Kumar and Chitra. He'd noticed it subtly at first, a slight hesitation in her smile, a fleeting shadow in her eyes that vanished before he could fully grasp it. It wasn't a dramatic shift, not a sudden explosion of anger or a declaration of discontent. It was a slow, insidious erosion, like the relentless drip of water wearing away at stone.

Chitra, usually so vibrant and full of life, had become quieter, more withdrawn. Her usual boisterous laughter, a sound that had once filled their small rented room with warmth and joy, had become less frequent, replaced by a quietude that felt both unsettling and profound. He'd tried to attribute it to the pressure of her UPSC preparation, the relentless grind of studying, the weight of expectation, but a nagging feeling persisted that something more was at play. The hours she spent poring over books seemed longer, the silences between them heavier, laden with an unspoken weight that Kumar couldn't quite decipher.

He recalled a recent evening, a seemingly ordinary night. They were sitting on their worn-out charpoy, reviewing her notes, the dim light of a single bulb casting long shadows on the wall. He'd been explaining a particularly complex section on constitutional law, his voice low and earnest. He'd paused, expecting her usual lively questions or insightful comments, but she simply nodded, her gaze distant, her eyes unfocused. It wasn't just a lack of engagement; it was an absence, a void that echoed in the silence between them.

Another instance stood out: a casual invitation to attend a movie, one he'd chosen carefully, a light-hearted comedy to provide a much-needed break from their studies. She'd accepted initially, with a hesitant smile that didn't quite reach her eyes. Later, she'd suggested rescheduling, citing a sudden surge in her workload. It wasn't a blatant rejection; it was a gentle deflection, a subtle avoidance that left Kumar feeling confused and unsettled. The casual ease of their early days together seemed to have faded, replaced by a hesitant politeness, a careful dance around unspoken feelings.

The small gestures, the seemingly insignificant details, had taken on a new significance. He'd noticed she'd stopped leaving little notes for him on the kitchen table, those whimsical messages that used to brighten his day. The shared cup of chai in the evenings, once a cherished ritual, now felt almost perfunctory, the warmth of the beverage unable to penetrate the chill that had settled between them. The touch of her hand, once so readily offered, now felt less frequent, replaced by a polite but distant acknowledgment. He'd tried to initiate conversations, to bridge the growing gap, but his attempts often felt forced, clumsy, like trying to build a bridge with broken planks. His carefully chosen words seemed to hang in the air, unanswered, unacknowledged. He'd ask about her day, her studies, her mood, but her responses were brief, perfunctory, lacking the usual enthusiasm and warmth.

Even her physical presence seemed to have changed. The usual sparkle in her eyes, the lively glint of intelligence and wit, seemed dimmed, clouded over by an unseen weariness. Her laughter, once infectious, felt muted, distant, like the echo of a fading memory. There was a fragility to her now, a vulnerability that both captivated and worried him. He'd reach out to touch her arm, offer words of comfort or encouragement, but his touch often felt rebuffed, his words falling flat, lost in the emotional chasm that had developed between them.

He questioned himself, his own behavior, his own actions. Had he been neglecting her? Had his preoccupation with studies and work led him to overlook her needs, her

feelings? Had he unintentionally pushed her away with his own anxieties and struggles? The self-doubt gnawed at him, adding to the already overwhelming pressure of his academic life and his financial constraints.

He reminisced about their first encounter, the innocent laughter, the shared dreams, the budding affection that had blossomed into a deep and abiding love. The memories played out in his mind, a vivid montage of shared joy and unspoken promises. He'd felt a profound connection with Chitra, a spiritual affinity that transcended the mundane realities of their lives. He'd believed they were building something special, something enduring, something that would weather any storm. But now, the storm was here, and he was unsure whether their love was strong enough to withstand it.

The unspoken questions hung heavy in the air: was this a temporary phase, a blip in their relationship, or was it something more profound, a growing divergence of paths? He found himself analyzing her every word, every gesture, searching for clues, for answers, for a hint of the spark that had once burned so brightly between them. The city, once a shared aspiration, now seemed to be a barrier, a silent witness to their growing distance. He wondered if their shared dreams were becoming fragmented, splintering like a fallen mirror.

He realized that even the simplest act, like sharing a meal, had lost its intimacy. The clinking of cutlery, the sound of their quiet conversation, once comforting, now felt strained and hollow. The silences between them were no longer comfortable, no longer the quiet understanding of two souls intertwined, but tense, ominous pauses, filled with unspoken accusations and unresolved tensions.

Kumar was aware that he needed to confront Chitra, to talk about their growing distance, to address the unspoken feelings that hung between them like a suffocating shroud. But he also felt a hesitation, a fear of disrupting the fragile equilibrium, of pushing her further away. He was caught in a delicate balance, unsure how to approach her, fearful of revealing the anxieties that gnawed at him. He knew that silence would only amplify their growing distance, but the fear of confrontation paralyzed him, leaving him in a state of limbo, suspended between hope and despair. The weight of his own unspoken anxieties and her subtle withdrawal added to the already overwhelming pressure of his city life. He knew he couldn't let things continue this way, but he was lost in the labyrinth of their unspoken words, desperately seeking a way out.

The scent of jasmine, usually a fragrant reminder of Chitra's favorite perfume, now seemed to carry a different note, a hint of something artificial, something subtly off. It was a small thing, easily dismissed, but it added to the growing unease that had taken root in Kumar's heart. He noticed she started staying out late, often returning after midnight, her explanations vague and unconvincing. The usual playful banter over dinner was replaced by rushed meals, eaten in silence, punctuated only by the clatter of utensils. He'd try to engage her in conversation, to inquire about her day, but her responses were clipped, her gaze averted.

He remembered a particular evening, a Tuesday, if his memory served him right. He'd been meticulously preparing for his own exams, the weight of his own academic pressures a constant companion. He looked up to see Chitra on the phone, her voice low and hushed. She quickly ended the call when he looked over, a slight flush colouring her cheeks. The casual ease with which she'd once shared details of her day, her friends, her studies, was gone, replaced by a guardedness that felt both painful and puzzling. He'd asked casually who she was talking to, a seemingly innocent question. Her response was a noncommittal, “Oh, just a friend,” delivered with an unconvincing smile that failed to reach her eyes.

The "friend" became a recurring theme. Late-night calls, hushed conversations, cryptic messages – the evidence, though circumstantial, was accumulating, forming a disturbing mosaic of secrecy. His attempts to rationalize her behavior, to attribute it to stress, to the intense pressure of her UPSC preparation, were becoming increasingly difficult to sustain. The nagging suspicion that something was amiss burrowed deeper, taking root in his mind like a persistent weed.

He found himself scrutinizing her belongings, a behaviour entirely out of character for him. He wasn’t a jealous or possessive person; he trusted Chitra implicitly, or at least, he *had* trusted her implicitly. But the mounting evidence, the subtle shifts in her behaviour, were chipping away at his confidence, leaving him feeling vulnerable and insecure. He'd find her purse open, her phone lying carelessly on the table, a strange impulse pushing him to look, to see what he shouldn't see. He'd quickly dismiss the impulse, chastising himself for his paranoia. But the doubt lingered, a persistent shadow clinging to the edges of his thoughts.

He started noticing small details: the new perfume, a scent he didn't recognize; a stray hair on her sweater, a dark brown, distinctly different from her own jet-black hair; the expensive pen, a Montblanc, that appeared out of nowhere. These were minor things, inconsequential in themselves, but in the context of her increasingly evasive behaviour, they took on a sinister significance. They were like bread crumbs, scattered along a path he wasn't sure he wanted to follow.

The city, once a shared dream, a beacon of hope and opportunity, now felt like a vast, indifferent landscape, a place where secrets could easily be hidden, and where a person could disappear without a trace. The anonymity of urban life, which had once been a thrilling aspect of their transition from rural India, now felt menacing, a suffocating cloak of secrecy.

His nights were filled with restless sleep, haunted by fragmented images and nagging doubts. He replayed conversations in his mind, searching for hidden meanings, for subtle cues that he'd missed. He analyzed her tone, her body language, the infinitesimal shifts in her expression, searching for clues to unravel the mystery that was consuming him. He was caught in a vortex of suspicion, his mind racing, his heart heavy with a mixture of love, fear, and betrayal.

He tried to talk to her, to initiate a conversation, to broach the subject of her late nights and secretive phone calls. But his attempts were met with defensiveness, with evasive answers, with a wall of silence that seemed insurmountable. The fear of pushing her further away, of jeopardizing their relationship, held him back. He was caught in a delicate dance between his growing suspicion and his desperate desire to maintain their fragile equilibrium. He felt like he was walking on eggshells, constantly on the verge of shattering the illusion of their perfect love story.

His attempts to rationalize her behavior were becoming increasingly strained. He'd convince himself that it was just the pressure of the UPSC exams, the demanding nature of her studies, the sheer weight of expectations. But deep down, he knew that something wasn't right. He'd remember their early days, filled with carefree laughter, shared dreams, a love that seemed invincible. He'd recall the innocent affection, the stolen kisses, the quiet moments of intimacy, and these memories would clash sharply with the present reality, highlighting the growing chasm that was tearing them apart.

The love he felt for Chitra was profound, a deep and abiding love that had been forged in the crucible of their shared experiences. But this love was now interwoven with a growing sense of betrayal, a creeping doubt that was slowly poisoning their relationship. He knew he couldn't continue to live in this state of uncertainty, of agonizing suspicion. He needed to confront his fears, to face the truth, whatever it might be. The question was: how could he do so without destroying everything they had built together? The weight of this question hung heavy in the air, as heavy as the unspoken words that hung between them, a silent testament to the cracks that were beginning to appear in their once-perfect façade. The city lights, once a symbol of hope and promise, now seemed to mock him with their cold, indifferent glow. The jasmine perfume, once so comforting, now stung his senses with the bitter scent of unspoken betrayal. The future, once so bright and full of promise, now felt uncertain, clouded by the shadow of his growing suspicion.

The next morning, the city's relentless hum felt particularly abrasive. The usual comforting rhythm of urban life – the distant sirens, the rumble of traffic, the chatter of vendors – now grated on Kumar's nerves, mirroring the turmoil within him. He had spent a sleepless night, the ghost of Chitra's unconvincing smile haunting his dreams. He knew he couldn't postpone it any longer. He had to confront her.

He found her in the kitchen, her back to him, humming a tuneless melody as she prepared breakfast. The sight of her, so seemingly ordinary, so effortlessly domestic, made the task ahead even harder. The scent of freshly brewed coffee, usually a welcome aroma, now felt suffocating, heavy with the weight of his unspoken accusations.

He cleared his throat, the sound echoing unnaturally loud in the small apartment. Chitra turned, her face betraying a flicker of surprise, quickly masked by a practiced composure. She offered a weak smile, a fragile imitation of her usual radiant cheer. It was this manufactured smile that finally shattered the dam of his restraint.

"Chitra," he began, his voice trembling slightly, "we need to talk."

The words hung in the air, heavy with unspoken anxieties. He watched as the colour drained from her face, the forced cheerfulness melting away to reveal a stark, underlying vulnerability. He saw a flicker of fear in her eyes, a fleeting moment of truth that only served to intensify his apprehension.

He sat down heavily at the kitchen table, the weight of his own emotions pressing down on him. He watched her nervously fidget with a spoon, her hands trembling slightly. The silence stretched, punctuated only by the rhythmic ticking of the kitchen clock, each tick amplifying the tension between them.

He plunged into the conversation, his voice a low, urgent murmur. He didn't launch into accusations; he simply laid out the facts as he saw them: the late nights, the hushed phone calls, the subtle changes in her demeanor, the expensive pen that had inexplicably appeared, the unfamiliar perfume. Each point he raised felt like a blow, striking at the very foundation of their relationship. He spoke of the gnawing uncertainty, the sleepless nights, the agonizing doubts that had slowly poisoned their once-perfect love. He spoke of the deep, abiding love he felt for her, a love that was now inextricably intertwined with a crushing sense of betrayal.

Chitra listened without interrupting, her gaze fixed on the table, her face a mask of controlled emotion. He waited for denial, for anger, for a flood of excuses. But none came. When he finally fell silent, she remained still, a statue of quiet resignation.

Finally, she spoke, her voice barely a whisper, barely audible above the city's persistent hum. "Kumar," she began, her voice laced with a pain that mirrored his own. "There's something I need to tell you." And then, she confessed.

She didn't offer excuses or justifications. She simply recounted the story, her voice shaking with a mixture of shame and sorrow. She spoke of the pressures of the UPSC exams, the crushing weight of expectations, the loneliness that had crept into their lives amidst the chaos of the city. She spoke of a chance encounter, a fleeting moment of weakness, a brief lapse in judgment. She confessed to a brief affair, a whirlwind romance that had been fueled by vulnerability and desperation. It was not a grand, passionate love story; it was a messy, complicated entanglement born out of a moment of weakness. She spoke of regret, of shame, and of a deep, profound remorse for the hurt she had caused.

Kumar listened in stunned silence, his heart slowly cracking under the weight of her confession. The words, once whispered, now echoed in the silence, each one a blow to his soul. The pain was raw, visceral, a physical ache that tightened his chest. His world, once a vibrant tapestry woven with shared dreams and promises, was now crumbling, the threads dissolving into dust.

He felt a wave of nausea wash over him, a sickening mixture of anger, betrayal, and a profound sense of loss. The city outside, with its incessant noise and activity, seemed to fade into the background as the reality of her confession settled upon him. His earlier anxieties had been replaced by a cold, hollow certainty. The fragile equilibrium he had so desperately tried to maintain had shattered, leaving him standing on the precipice of a devastating heartbreak.

The silence stretched between them, a chasm filled with unspoken accusations and unbearable grief. He looked at her, his love for her now tangled with a deep, stinging resentment. The image of their early days, filled with laughter and shared dreams, felt like a distant, almost unreal memory. He felt the sting of betrayal, a violation so profound that it threatened to swallow him whole.

He remained silent for what seemed like an eternity, absorbing the magnitude of what she had confessed. The coffee, still steaming on the table, seemed to mock him with its warmth, a stark contrast to the icy chill that had settled deep within his bones. The apartment, once a sanctuary of love and shared happiness, now felt like a cold, empty space, devoid of warmth and affection. The city lights, which had once represented a beacon of hope and opportunity, now seemed to mock him with their indifferent glow.

He struggled to find words, to articulate the torrent of emotions that were surging through him. The pain was so overwhelming, so all-encompassing, that it was almost paralyzing. He wanted to scream, to rage, to lash out. But all he could manage was a single, barely audible question.

“Why, Chitra? Why?”

The question hung in the air, raw and accusatory, yet filled with a desperate plea for understanding. Chitra’s response was a silent sob, a tremor in her voice, a silent confession of her own pain, a silent acknowledgment of the irreparable damage she had caused. The confrontation had ended, but the true pain, the slow agonizing unraveling of their relationship, was only just beginning. The cracks in their façade, once subtle and almost imperceptible, had now widened into a gaping chasm, leaving their future uncertain and their love in ruins. The city, once a symbol of their shared hopes and dreams, now seemed to conspire in their unspoken sorrow, a silent witness to the disintegration of their once-perfect love story.

The silence that followed Chitra's confession was deafening, a void that swallowed the city's usual cacophony. The rhythmic tick-tock of the kitchen clock became a morbid metronome, each beat a hammer blow against the fragile remnants of Kumar's heart. He stared at her, at the woman he had loved with a fierceness that had seemed unshakeable, and saw only a stranger, etched with a sorrow that mirrored his own, yet felt utterly alien. The Chitra he knew, the vibrant, spirited woman who had shared his dreams of a life beyond the dusty lanes of his village, was gone, replaced by a ghost of her former self, haunted by guilt and regret.

He reached for his coffee, the warmth of the mug a stark contrast to the icy chill that had settled deep within his soul. The rich aroma, once a comfort, now felt like a cruel mockery, a reminder of the shared moments that were now irrevocably tainted. He took a sip, the bitterness a perfect reflection of the truth that had been laid bare. The city, once a symbol of their shared aspirations, now felt like a cold, indifferent observer, a vast, impersonal entity that had swallowed his happiness whole.

The memories flooded back – the bustling railway station, the chaotic yet exhilarating journey to the city, the shared excitement of finding their small apartment, the quiet evenings spent studying, the stolen moments of laughter amidst the relentless pressure of city life. Each memory, once a vibrant jewel, now seemed tarnished, coated in a layer of disillusionment. The future they had painstakingly constructed, brick by brick, dream by dream, lay in ruins, reduced to a pile of rubble under the weight of Chitra's confession.

His mind raced, a whirlwind of emotions – anger, betrayal, confusion, a deep, gnawing sense of loss. He wanted to lash out, to scream, to break something, anything, to shatter the silence that pressed down on him like a physical weight. But the words caught in his throat, choked by a rising tide of despair. He felt utterly alone, adrift in a sea of grief, the city lights blurring into a meaningless smear through his tear-filled eyes.

He thought of his family back home, their unwavering belief in his success, their pride in his city life, their faith in his relationship with Chitra. The thought of having to break the news to them, of explaining the devastation that had befallen him, felt almost unbearable. How could he convey the depth of his pain, the shattering of his carefully constructed world, to people who had placed their hopes and dreams in his hands?

He looked at Chitra again, her eyes brimming with tears, her shoulders trembling with suppressed sobs. The anger that had threatened to consume him momentarily subsided, replaced by a weary compassion. He saw not a betrayer, but a woman broken by the pressures of a life she had perhaps not been fully prepared for. He saw a reflection of his own vulnerabilities, his own moments of weakness, his own struggles to navigate the complexities of the city and its relentless demands.

The city, with its relentless pulse, its constant noise, its anonymity, had played a role in their downfall. The pressure of the UPSC exams, the loneliness of navigating a new environment, the subtle erosion of their intimacy amidst the chaos of urban life – these were all contributing factors, a silent chorus to the tragedy unfolding before him. He understood, on some level, the circumstances that had led to her transgression, but that understanding did not lessen the pain. The wound was deep, the scar would likely be permanent.

He thought of the expensive pen, the unfamiliar perfume, the hushed phone calls, the late nights – the clues he had so desperately tried to ignore, the signs he had dismissed as insignificant anxieties. Now, they were stark reminders of his own naivety, his blindness to the truth that had been unfolding right under his nose. He had been so consumed by his own aspirations, so focused on achieving his dreams, that he had failed to see the cracks forming in the foundation of their relationship.

He had always believed in their love, a love that had blossomed amidst the poverty and simplicity of their village, a love that had sustained them through the challenges of their transition to the city. He had envisioned a life together, a future filled with shared dreams and mutual support. Now, that future was a mirage, a shimmering illusion that had dissolved into thin air, leaving him stranded in the harsh reality of betrayal and heartbreak.

The city, with its millions of stories, its millions of lives, felt less like a place of opportunity and more like a vast, indifferent landscape, a silent witness to the disintegration of his happiness. He had arrived in the city with hopes high, dreams bright, and a love that he thought was unbreakable. Now, he was left with nothing but the bitter taste of betrayal, the aching emptiness of a broken heart, and the cold, harsh reality of his situation.

The hours that followed were filled with a silence heavier than any words could express. They sat in the kitchen, the remnants of their breakfast long forgotten, the city's relentless hum a constant background to their unspoken grief. The light of dawn seeped into the apartment, illuminating the emptiness in their eyes, the desolation in their hearts. The cracks in their façade were no longer subtle; they were gaping chasms, threatening to swallow them whole. Their love story, once a vibrant testament to their shared dreams, had become a tale of betrayal, a haunting melody played on the strings of a broken heart, in the heart of a city that offered no solace, no comfort, only the indifferent glare of its million lights. The future loomed uncertain, an uncharted territory filled with an unknown mix of grief, pain, and the daunting task of picking up the pieces of a life shattered beyond repair. The city, once a symbol of their aspirations, now felt like a vast, indifferent prison, holding them captive in the aftermath of their devastating heartbreak. The bitter truth, sharp and unavoidable, hung heavy in the air between them, a silent testament to the collapse of their perfect love story.

The train rattled, a metallic symphony of clanking wheels and groaning metal, mirroring the discordant rhythm of Kumar's heart. He stared out the window, the city's blurred lights gradually giving way to the familiar darkness of the countryside. The cityscape, once a beacon of hope, now felt like a distant, cruel memory. Each passing field, each fleeting glimpse of a village home, stirred a complex mix of emotions – relief, sadness, a profound sense of failure. He was returning, not as the triumphant son his family expected, but as a broken man, his dreams shattered, his heart wounded.

The air grew cooler, fresher, the scent of damp earth and woodsmoke replacing the city's acrid mix of exhaust fumes and cheap perfume. A nostalgic pang resonated within him, a wave of memory washing over him – the scent of his mother's cooking, the familiar songs of the village, the comforting weight of his father's hand on his shoulder. These were the anchors of his past, the touchstones he had so eagerly left behind in his pursuit of urban success, only to discover they were the very things he desperately needed now.

The journey was a slow, agonizing stripping away of the layers of city life he had meticulously constructed – the tailored suits, the polished shoes, the sophisticated vocabulary, the carefully cultivated air of success. Each passing mile seemed to peel away another layer, revealing the vulnerable, heartbroken man beneath. The meticulously curated facade of urban life crumbled like dried clay under the relentless onslaught of his grief. He had arrived in the city clutching tightly to his dreams and a heart filled with love, and he was now returning with only the wreckage of his aspirations and a gaping void where his heart used to be.

He watched the landscape transform – from the sprawling concrete jungle to the gentle undulations of green paddy fields, the stark contrast a mirror of the internal upheaval within him. The rhythmic chugging of the train became a mournful counterpoint to the silent turmoil in his soul. He closed his eyes, allowing the memories to flood back – the initial euphoria of arriving in the city, the exhilaration of newfound independence, the excitement of shared dreams with Chitra. Now, these memories were tainted, bitter reminders of a love lost, a future shattered.

The train slowed, the rhythmic chugging subsiding to a gentle groan as it approached the station. His heart pounded in his chest, a frantic drumbeat against the silence of the carriage. He knew he couldn't delay the inevitable. He had to face his family, to confront the disappointment, the hurt, the shattering of their carefully nurtured hopes. He had carried the burden of his failure, his heartbreak, alone for far too long. The weight of it had pressed down upon him, crushing him beneath its heavy load. The weight of expectation had been an invisible burden he'd carried with him throughout his journey, a burden of silent promises and unspoken dreams. But now, the weight of his failure was too much to bear alone. He had to share it.

He stepped onto the platform, the familiar scent of dust and earth filling his lungs. The station, once a gateway to his dreams, now felt like a return to reality, a harsh reminder of the chasm that separated his aspirations from his reality. The air seemed charged with expectation, a palpable tension that amplified his apprehension. He could almost feel the weight of his parents' hopes and dreams pressing down on him. He had been their golden boy, the one who had escaped the shackles of poverty and the limitations of their village life. Now, what would they think of their broken son?

As he stepped out of the station, a wave of memories washed over him. The sounds, the smells, the familiar faces – a tapestry of his past life unfurled before him. Children chased after stray dogs, women gossiped in hushed tones, men engaged in casual conversations by the roadside tea stall. Life continued, its rhythm undisturbed by his personal tragedy, a stark contrast to the tumultuous storm raging within him. He felt a pang of both comfort and isolation. The familiar setting was a balm to his bruised soul, yet he was acutely aware of his aloneness.

His home was a humble dwelling, a stark contrast to the sleek city apartment he had recently vacated. Yet, as he approached, a strange sense of peace settled over him. It wasn't the grandeur of the urban landscape but the simplicity of the countryside that soothed his soul. The familiarity of his surroundings, the comfort of his childhood home, offered a semblance of solace, a haven amidst the devastation of his loss.

His parents were waiting for him, their faces etched with a mixture of anticipation and concern. He could see the questions in their eyes, the unspoken hopes hanging heavy in the air. How could he possibly articulate the pain he carried within, the depth of his despair, the cruel reality of his shattered dreams? How could he explain the betrayal, the loss, the gaping hole in his heart?

The ensuing days were a blur of forced smiles, strained conversations, and a heavy silence that hung like a shroud over their home. His parents, though clearly heartbroken by the news of his failed relationship, tried their best to offer comfort and support. Their love, unwavering and steadfast, was a lifeline in his sea of grief. He found solace in their familiar routines, in the simplicity of village life, in the quiet moments of shared meals and evening conversations.

The fields stretched out before him, vast and unending, mirroring the seemingly endless expanse of his grief. He spent hours walking through the familiar paths, his feet finding the worn tracks, his body unconsciously returning to the rhythm of his youth. The familiar sights and sounds of the village acted as a gentle balm to his wounded soul, a silent solace in the face of his loss. The quiet hum of the countryside was a stark contrast to the relentless noise of the city, a calming counterpoint to the tempest in his heart.

He found himself drawn to the river, its steady flow a calming presence in his turbulent world. He watched as the water flowed smoothly, its course never faltering, its rhythm unperturbed by obstacles or turmoil. The river, a timeless symbol of life and continuity, offered a silent lesson in acceptance, resilience, and the unyielding march of time.

His return to the village was not merely a physical journey; it was a profound emotional pilgrimage, a return to the roots of his being. It was a journey of self-reflection, a painful process of confronting his failures, his mistakes, his vulnerabilities. It was a slow, gradual unburdening of his grief, a quiet letting go. The city had offered him dreams of success, of a life beyond his wildest imagination, but it had also taken away his heart, leaving him with a void that only the familiarity of his roots could begin to fill. The journey back to his village was the first step in his long and arduous process of healing, a testament to his strength, a promise to himself to reclaim his life, to rebuild his dreams, and to find peace amidst the wreckage of his past. The future remained uncertain, filled with the unknown, but he found comfort in the simple, unwavering embrace of his village and the steadfast love of his family.

The return journey wasn't just a return to his home; it was a return to himself.

Chapter 3

Where Love Wears Dust

"प्रेम में वफिल होना जीवन की सबसे बड़ी सीख है।"

-Amrita Pritam

(To fail in love is to receive life's most profound lesson.)

The scent of woodsmoke and damp earth, a perfume he'd almost forgotten, wrapped around him like a comforting blanket. The city's cacophony was replaced by the gentle chirping of crickets and the rustling of leaves – a symphony of nature that soothed his frayed nerves. His small, mud-brick home, once a symbol of limitations, now felt like a sanctuary, a haven from the relentless storm raging within him. The familiar worn wooden door, the slightly crooked window frames, the scent of his mother's turmeric-infused cooking – these were not just objects; they were the anchors of his past, the threads of his identity that had been frayed but not broken.

His parents, their faces etched with worry lines softened by the warmth of their love, greeted him with a silent embrace. There were no grand pronouncements, no accusations, only the unspoken understanding that transcended words. His mother's touch, gentle and reassuring, felt like a balm on his wounded soul. His father, a man of few words, sat beside him, his presence a silent testament to his unwavering support. The weight of expectation, the invisible burden he had carried for so long, seemed to lift slightly under the weight of their unconditional love. He saw a flicker of pain in their eyes; they were hurting too, bearing the silent burden of his failure, silently sharing in his grief.

The village itself was a balm. The rhythmic sway of the paddy fields in the gentle breeze, the rhythmic thud of the village blacksmith's hammer, the cheerful chatter of women drawing water from the well – these were the components of a life he had once dismissed as mundane, but now they resonated with a newfound beauty. The simplicity of existence, devoid of the city's frantic pace and relentless competition, offered a profound sense of peace.

Days melted into weeks, each sunrise painting the sky in hues of hope he hadn't dared to feel in the city. He found himself spending hours wandering through the familiar paths, his feet instinctively knowing the way, his body remembering the rhythm of his youth. He revisited his old haunts – the banyan tree under which he had spent countless hours reading, the riverbank where he had played as a child, the small temple where he had prayed for his dreams. Each place held a memory, a fragment of his past, each one contributing to the slow process of healing.

He helped his father in the fields, the physical exertion a welcome distraction from the turmoil in his mind. The smell of the freshly turned earth, the feel of the sun on his skin, the camaraderie of his fellow villagers these were tangible reminders of a life grounded in reality, in connection, in community. The work was hard, the sun relentless, but it was honest work, honest living. And it was a stark contrast to the artificiality of his city life, the superficiality of relationships, the constant striving for something always just out of reach.

Evenings were spent under the starry sky, listening to his grandfather's stories, stories woven with the magic of folklore and the wisdom of generations. The narratives, simple yet profound, offered a different perspective on life, on love, on loss. They spoke of resilience, of acceptance, of the cyclical nature of life and death, of hope blossoming even in the bleakest of landscapes. The elders' presence was an anchor; their quiet wisdom, a lighthouse guiding him through the stormy seas of his grief.

The quiet mornings, filled with the sounds of nature awakening, were his meditative moments. He watched the sunrise paint the sky in vibrant colours, each shade a promise of a new beginning. He learned to listen to the silent language of nature, to appreciate the delicate dance between light and shadow, to find beauty in the simplicity of existence. The slow, deliberate pace of village life offered a respite from the city's relentless pressure, a space to breathe, to reflect, to heal.

He rediscovered the small joys he had overlooked in his city life – the sweetness of mangoes plucked fresh from the tree, the taste of his mother's home-cooked meals, the warmth of a bonfire on a chilly evening, the comforting presence of family gathered around, sharing stories and laughter. These simple pleasures, once taken for granted, now felt like precious gifts, reminders of the beauty of life's everyday moments

One afternoon, he found himself by the river, watching the water flow, its currents mirroring the ebb and flow of his emotions. He remembered Chitra, their shared dreams, their love, and the pain of her betrayal. The memories weren't as sharp as they once were, the edges softened by the passage of time and the healing balm of his village. He realized that his grief wasn't a sign of weakness but a testament to the depth of his love, a measure of the intensity of his emotions.

He understood, with a clarity that came only from the quiet solitude of the village, that moving on wasn't about forgetting but about accepting, about integrating the pain into the narrative of his life, allowing it to shape him without defining him. The city had offered him the illusion of success, a fleeting taste of glamour, but the village had offered him something far more valuable – a sense of belonging, a grounding in reality, a pathway to healing.

His return to the village wasn't a retreat from life; it was a strategic repositioning, a necessary step towards reclaiming his own narrative. It was a conscious choice to embrace simplicity, to find strength in his roots, to heal from the wounds of the past, and to pave the way for a future defined by his own terms, not by the expectations of the city or the illusions of an unattainable dream.

The weight on his shoulders, the invisible burden of expectations and failure, had begun to lift, replaced by a quiet sense of peace, a deep-seated understanding of self, and a renewed sense of purpose. He realized that healing wasn't a linear journey, that there were good days and bad days, moments of clarity and moments of doubt. But the village, with its gentle rhythm and unwavering embrace, provided the sanctuary he needed to navigate those ups and downs, to find his footing, and to start rebuilding his life, one brick at a time, one sunrise at a time.

He realized that true success wasn't measured in material possessions or professional achievements, but in the strength of one's spirit, the depth of one's relationships, and the peace found in the simple rhythms of life. And in the heart of his village, surrounded by the familiar scents, sounds, and faces of his past, he began to envision a future that wasn't defined by loss but by growth, a future filled with the promise of a love that was real, a success that was authentic, and a happiness that was deeply rooted in the simple joys of life. The village wasn't just a place; it was the beginning of his new journey – a journey back to himself. The city had taken a lot from him, but it hadn't taken his strength, his resilience, or the deep-seated love for his family and roots. And that was enough. That was more than enough. It was everything.

The rhythmic creak of the old wooden swing under the mango tree became the soundtrack to his afternoons. He'd sit there, watching his younger sister, Maya, her laughter a bright melody against the backdrop of the rustling leaves. He hadn't realized how much he'd missed the simple joy of her presence, the uncomplicated affection of a sibling's bond. He'd join her in her games, feeling a lightness in his heart he hadn't experienced in months. The city had stolen so much, but it hadn't managed to erode the love that bound him to his family.

Evenings were spent by the flickering lamplight, listening to his grandfather's stories, tales spun from the rich tapestry of village life, folklore, and ancient wisdom. The stories were not just narratives; they were lessons, whispered secrets of resilience, patience, and the enduring strength of the human spirit. They spoke of love found and lost, of betrayals and forgiveness, of the cyclical nature of life, mirroring his own journey in ways he hadn't fully understood until now. His grandfather's gnarled hands, etched with the map of a life lived fully, held his own with a reassuring firmness. Those hands had tilled the land, built their home, raised a family. They spoke of a strength that resonated deeply within Kumar.

The village women, their hands as weathered as the earth they worked, welcomed him with open arms. Their shared laughter over morning chai, their quiet camaraderie as they worked together in the fields, were small acts of kindness that soothed his soul. They didn't pry into his past; their acceptance was a comforting balm. He found himself participating in their daily routines, learning the nuances of their world, the intricate dance of their social fabric. He learned to distinguish the different calls of the birds, the subtle changes in the weather through the clouds, the rhythm of the seasons in the rustling paddy fields. It was a world of details, of textures, and subtle harmonies; a world he had been blind to in the city's relentless pursuit of success.

He began to find solace in the mundane tasks – the rhythmic weeding of the fields, the meticulous planting of seeds, the gentle process of harvesting. These weren't just physical acts; they were meditative practices, allowing him to quiet his mind, to connect with the earth, to feel the slow, steady rhythm of life. The sun on his skin, the earth under his feet, the quiet companionship of his father, all contributed to a growing sense of peace, of groundedness, of belonging. The physical exertion became a cathartic release, transforming the anger and frustration into productive energy.

One day, he found himself sketching the village, capturing the essence of its charm in his notebook. He'd always been a keen observer, and now he found himself noticing things he'd never seen before - the play of light and shadow on the mud walls, the intricate patterns in the woven baskets, the expressive eyes of the village animals. His sketches weren't mere representations; they were emotional expressions, capturing the quiet beauty of the village, his emotions finding an outlet through the strokes of his pencil. He rediscovered his creative passion, a hidden wellspring of energy he hadn't realized was still there.

He spent hours reading, losing himself in the pages of books under the shade of the old banyan tree. It was a familiar ritual, a comforting routine that transported him to other worlds, offering respite from his own reality. He found himself drawn to literature exploring themes of loss, healing, and renewal, finding parallels in the narratives that resonated with his own experience. The books weren't escapes; they were companions, guiding him through his emotional labyrinth.

His mother's cooking became a source of profound comfort. The familiar aromas of turmeric, ginger, and chili filled his senses, evoking childhood memories, a sense of warmth and security. Each meal was more than sustenance; it was an act of love, a tangible expression of her unwavering support. He found himself lingering at the table, savoring the flavors, appreciating the simplicity and heartfulness of his mother's cooking, the uncomplicated gesture of her providing for him, a gesture that had always felt so ordinary and had become deeply meaningful now.

The healing wasn't instantaneous. There were days when the memories of Chitra, the pain of betrayal, would rise to the surface, threatening to engulf him once more. But the village, in its quiet strength, offered him a space to process his emotions, to grieve without judgment. He learned to allow himself to feel the pain, to accept it as a part of his journey, without letting it define him. He started to recognize the cycles of his grief, the ebb and flow of his emotions, understanding that they were transient, not permanent.

He discovered the soothing power of silence. He learned to appreciate the quiet moments, the stillness between the sounds, the peace that came with simply being. He practiced mindfulness, focusing on his breath, on the sensations of his body, on the present moment. The village offered him a space to be still, to listen to the inner whispers of his heart, to connect with his deepest self.

He began to journal, chronicling his journey of healing, pouring out his thoughts and emotions onto the page. Writing became a way of processing his experiences, of making sense of his own story. It was a form of self-expression, a means of understanding himself, of forging a new identity, one that was rooted in self-acceptance and self-compassion. He started small, with brief entries, but as the weeks passed, the writings became longer, more insightful, reflecting the progress he was making, the growing clarity of his thinking, his evolving understanding of life's nuances.
The simple act of walking through the paddy fields, watching the sun rise and set over the horizon, became a ritual, a meditation in movement. He found a beauty in the simplicity of nature, a profound connection to the earth and its rhythms. He was reconnecting to his roots, not just literally but also figuratively, re-establishing his link to his cultural heritage, his identity and his very being.

One evening, as he sat with his family around a bonfire, he felt a profound sense of peace, a quiet understanding that his healing was not a destination but a process, a continuous unfolding of self. He was not the same person who had left the city, broken and disillusioned. He was stronger, wiser, more grounded, more self-aware. He had discovered a resilience within himself, a capacity for love and empathy that had been masked by the city's relentless pursuit of external validation. The village hadn't simply healed him; it had transformed him. He carried the scars of his past, but they were now badges of honor, a testament to his journey, to his strength, to his ability to rise from the ashes. He was ready to face the future, not with the naive optimism of his younger self, but with a quiet confidence, a grounded perspective, and a heart open to the

possibility of a love that was authentic, meaningful, and enduring. The city held a certain allure, he understood, but he would only return when he was truly ready, no longer driven by ambition but by a clear purpose and a newfound sense of self. For now, the village, with its gentle rhythm and profound solace, was his sanctuary, his home, and the perfect place to begin his new life.

The scent of jasmine and the distant call to prayer drifted on the morning air, a familiar rhythm that had become the soundtrack to his days. He watched his father, his silhouette framed against the rising sun as he performed his morning rituals at the village temple, a serene picture of devotion and calm. The rhythmic chants, the quiet reverence, the sense of community – it was all profoundly affecting. For the first time since his painful departure from the city, a flicker of something new ignited within him, a spark of purpose, of direction.

He'd always admired his father. Not just for his unwavering faith, but for the quiet dignity with which he served his community, his gentle kindness extending to everyone, regardless of their caste or creed. He was the heart of the village, a pillar of strength and compassion. Kumar had never truly understood the depth of his father's vocation, the profound impact he had on the lives he touched, until now.

One evening, as they sat together on the porch, the familiar clink of chai cups in the background, his father spoke of the priesthood. It wasn't a lecture or a suggestion; it was a shared contemplation, a quiet acknowledgment of the path that lay before him. He spoke of the responsibilities, the sacrifices, the immense satisfaction derived from serving God and his people. He described it not as a burden but as a privilege, a calling that filled his life with meaning and purpose.

Kumar listened intently, the words weaving a tapestry of possibility in his mind. He'd always been an artist, expressing himself through sketches and writings, but the city had stripped him of that passion, replacing it with a relentless pursuit of success that left him empty and broken. The village, however, had slowly rekindled that flame, encouraging a new kind of self-expression through his journal entries, through his observations of nature, through his quiet contemplation of the simple beauty surrounding him.

The idea of devoting his life to service, to helping others, began to resonate within him, a profound sense of purpose gradually replacing the emptiness he had carried for so long. It was a stark contrast to the cutthroat world of the city, a world where ambition and self-interest often overshadowed compassion and empathy. The tranquility of village life, the strong sense of community, the intricate network of relationships – all of it was helping him envision a life of meaning, of genuine connection.

He spent days observing his father, absorbing the nuances of his work, the quiet dignity with which he interacted with villagers seeking guidance and comfort. He watched as his father tirelessly offered solace to the grieving, counsel to those facing difficulties, and blessings to the hopeful. He noticed the reverence in the eyes of the villagers as they approached him, the unspoken trust and respect that he commanded.

He spent his evenings pouring over religious texts, ancient scriptures that echoed the stories his grandfather had told him. He discovered a rich tapestry of wisdom, lessons about compassion, forgiveness, and the importance of serving others. He found that this was not just a study of doctrines; it was a journey into the human heart, a study of our shared humanity, our universal struggles, and our unending search for meaning

He realized that his artistic talents could serve this calling. He could create artwork for the temple, capturing its beauty and spirituality in a way that inspired and uplifted those who sought refuge within its walls. He could use his words to teach the younger generation, preserving their rich cultural heritage and transmitting its wisdom to future generations. He envisioned himself incorporating his writing and sketching into his work as a priest, creating visual and narrative forms that helped amplify the spiritual teachings.

The city had been a harsh teacher, stripping him of his dreams and leaving him battered and bruised. But the village, with its quiet strength and unwavering support, had offered him a chance to heal, to rediscover himself, and to forge a new path, one that resonated deeply within his soul. This wasn't just about escaping the past; it was about embracing a future filled with purpose, a future where his artistic talents could be used to serve the community, a future where he could find peace and fulfillment in his work. The path ahead wouldn't be easy, he knew, but for the first time in a long time, he felt ready to embark on it with a sense of purpose, and a sense of hope

The decision wasn't a sudden epiphany; it was a gradual unfolding, a natural progression of his healing journey. It was a culmination of his experiences in the city, his rediscovery of himself in the village, his rekindling of his passion, and his newfound appreciation for the profound spiritual richness of his family's heritage. It represented a complete transformation in his outlook on life. It wasn't about escaping pain or hiding from the world anymore; it was about facing life's challenges with faith and resilience, about finding fulfillment in service, and about dedicating his life to something larger than himself.

The village had initially become a sanctuary, a place to heal and recover from the wounds of the past. Now, however, it was becoming a springboard for a new beginning, a launching point for a life deeply rooted in purpose and compassion. It became apparent to him that the wounds of the past, though painful, had shaped him, strengthened him, and ultimately led him to a path that felt perfectly aligned with his newfound self-understanding and spiritual awakening.

He pictured himself, not as a struggling artist in the bustling metropolis, perpetually chasing an elusive success, but as a respected member of his community, a beacon of hope and guidance, his life enriched by the simple act of service. He envisioned himself leading prayers, offering comfort, and using his artistic talents to spread faith and joy amongst his people. It was a life of quiet dignity, of profound meaning, and of deep personal satisfaction. He would still find solace in his art, but now, it would be infused with a deeper purpose, a powerful connection to the community he served. His past experiences would inform his future work, shaping his empathy and providing a unique lens through which to perceive and understand the lives of those around him.

He shared his thoughts with his mother, her eyes mirroring the pride and joy in his father's. Her embrace, warm and reassuring, conveyed an unspoken understanding, a silent acceptance of his new direction. He felt her love, strong and unwavering, a constant source of strength throughout his journey. He knew he had her support unconditionally, a comforting truth that eased his transition into this new chapter of his life. Her simple approval solidified his decision, giving him the courage and reassurance he needed to fully commit to this new calling.

He understood that this path was not a rejection of his past aspirations but a transformation of them. The intensity of his previous ambitions had led to disillusionment, but this new vocation offered a different kind of fulfillment, one rooted in community, faith, and service. It was a path that aligned perfectly with his rediscovered self, a path that offered purpose, connection, and a profound sense of peace. He finally felt that he was on a journey towards truly becoming the person he was always meant to be.

His journey had been one of healing, introspection, and self-discovery. He had found solace in the quiet strength of his village, rekindled his creative spirit, and rediscovered the profound connection to his roots. He had now chosen a life of service, a path that integrated his creative talents with his spiritual awakening, and a life filled with meaning and purpose. The scars of his past remained, but they were now a reminder of his journey, a testament to his resilience, and an integral part of the person he had become. He carried them not with shame or regret, but with a quiet pride, knowing that his past experiences had ultimately led him to find his true calling. His future was no longer shrouded in uncertainty but illuminated by the clarity of his purpose and the unwavering support of his family and community. His heart was at peace; he was ready to embark on his new path.

The early mornings were no longer filled with the anxious scramble of city life, the relentless pressure to achieve, to succeed. Instead, they unfolded slowly, serenely, like the unfurling of a lotus blossom. The rhythmic chanting from the village temple, once a mere background hum, now resonated deep within him, a comforting rhythm that mirrored the steady beat of his own heart. He found himself waking before sunrise, drawn to the temple, not out of obligation, but out of a profound desire to be a part of the community's shared devotion. He began assisting his father, initially with small tasks – tidying the temple grounds, arranging flowers, helping with the preparations for ceremonies. These simple acts weren't just chores; they were acts of service, small gestures of devotion that connected him to something larger than himself. The weight of expectation he'd carried in the city, the suffocating pressure to achieve worldly success, began to lift. He felt lighter, freer, more at ease with himself.

His artistic talents, once dormant, began to reawaken. He started sketching the intricate carvings on the temple walls, capturing the details with an almost reverent attention. The sketches, initially just for himself, evolved into vibrant depictions of religious scenes, capturing the essence of faith and devotion in a way that resonated deeply with the villagers. He began to paint murals on the temple walls, illustrating stories from the scriptures, transforming the temple into a visual tapestry of religious *narratives* He discovered that his art wasn't merely a form of self-expression anymore; it was a means of communication, a bridge connecting the ancient wisdom of the scriptures to the hearts and minds of the villagers. The vibrant colors, the expressive lines, the powerful imagery – they all spoke of faith, hope, and the unwavering strength of the human spirit. His art became a tangible expression of his newfound purpose, a way to serve his community, and to share the spiritual richness of his heritage with those around him. One evening, as he sat sketching beneath the shade of a banyan tree, a young boy approached him, his eyes wide with curiosity. He asked Kumar about the figures in his sketch, about the stories they represented. Kumar, surprised by the boy's keen interest, began to narrate the tales, weaving them into an engaging narrative that captured the boy's imagination. He saw the spark of understanding in the boy's eyes, the quiet reverence that filled his gaze. This was more rewarding than any artistic recognition he had ever received in the city.

The incident triggered a new idea. He began to conduct storytelling sessions for the children in the village, using his sketches and his words to bring the ancient scriptures to life. He crafted engaging narratives, making the stories relatable and accessible to the young minds. He discovered a natural aptitude for teaching, a talent he never knew he possessed. The children listened with rapt attention, their faces alight with wonder and excitement. He felt a deep sense of satisfaction, a profound fulfillment in sharing his knowledge and passion with them.

The village wasn't just a refuge; it was a vibrant, interconnected community, a place where every individual played a vital role. He noticed the intricate web of relationships that bound the villagers together, the mutual support and shared responsibilities that ensured the smooth functioning of their lives. The elders shared their wisdom; the younger generation eagerly sought guidance. There was a palpable sense of belonging, a profound connection that transcended individual aspirations and embraced the collective well-being. This was something he'd profoundly lacked in the anonymity of the city.

Kumar found himself participating in village events, helping with harvests, celebrating festivals, offering support during times of hardship. These weren't merely social gatherings; they were expressions of communal solidarity, testaments to the strength and resilience of the community spirit. He felt a sense of belonging, a profound connection to the people around him, a sense of shared purpose that had eluded him in the city's isolated, individualistic environment.

His days were filled with meaningful activity, his evenings with quiet contemplation. He spent time reflecting on his past, accepting his failures, and appreciating the lessons he had learned. He realized that his journey from the city to the village wasn't simply a geographical shift; it was a profound transformation of his inner self, a rediscovery of his identity and purpose. The city had taught him the harsh lessons of ambition and disappointment; the village, on the other hand, was teaching him the beauty of simplicity, the value of community, the profound satisfaction of serving others.

His relationship with his parents deepened. He spent more time with them, sharing his experiences, seeking their guidance, and appreciating their unwavering support. He found solace in their presence, a comforting familiarity that grounded him and reaffirmed his connection to his roots. He realised the true value of family, the unconditional love and support that had always been there, even when he was lost and adrift in the city

One day, an elderly woman approached him, her eyes filled with tears. She spoke of her ailing husband, her voice trembling with worry. Kumar listened patiently, offering words of comfort and assurance. He didn't offer medical advice; he offered empathy, understanding, and a reassuring presence. He sat with her, sharing her grief, offering a listening ear, and letting her know that she wasn't alone in her suffering. The simple act of being present, of offering solace and companionship, felt incredibly fulfilling. It was a small act of kindness, yet it brought a profound sense of purpose, a quiet satisfaction that surpassed any material gain he had ever sought.

He found that his artistic talents, combined with his newfound empathy and understanding, allowed him to connect with people on a deeper level. He created portraits of the villagers, capturing not only their physical features but also their unique personalities, their life stories etched into their faces. These portraits weren't just works of art; they were tributes to the individuals who made up the vibrant tapestry of his community. Each portrait was a story, a testament to the resilience and spirit of the people he served.

As months turned into years, Kumar became an integral part of the village life. He was no longer just a visitor, a displaced city dweller seeking refuge. He was a member of the community, contributing to its well-being, sharing his talents and his empathy, finding fulfillment in the simple acts of service. The scars of his past remained, but they were no longer a source of shame or regret. They were a reminder of his journey, a testament to his resilience, a profound testament to the transformative power of finding one's purpose, and accepting the healing process. He had found his place, his purpose, his peace. The village, once a temporary haven, had become his home, a place where he had not just healed, but truly thrived. The quiet strength of the community, the rhythm of village life, the profound connection to his roots, had guided him to a life filled with purpose, compassion, and an enduring sense of belonging. His heart, once burdened by the weight of unfulfilled ambitions, now beat steadily with a quiet joy, a profound sense of peace he had never known before.

The monsoon rains arrived, washing over the village in a torrent of life-giving water. The parched earth drank deeply, the fields transformed into vibrant green carpets, and the air filled with the intoxicating fragrance of wet soil and blossoming jasmine. Kumar watched the downpour from the verandah of his childhood home, a sense of profound peace settling over him. The relentless anxieties that had once plagued him, the gnawing uncertainties of city life, felt distant and unreal, like echoes fading into the storm's roar. He was home.

His days were now a tapestry woven with the threads of community life. He helped his father with the daily rituals at the temple, his movements fluid and practiced, his heart filled with a quiet devotion. The intricate carvings on the temple walls, once the subject of his sketches, now felt like familiar friends, their stories etched into his memory. He continued to paint murals, each stroke of his brush a prayer, each color a testament to his faith. The children still gathered around him, their eyes wide with wonder as he narrated tales from the scriptures, his voice resonating with the warmth of his newfound purpose.

His artistic talents had become a bridge, connecting the generations, preserving the rich cultural heritage of his village. He began teaching the older children traditional art forms, passing on the skills he had honed over the years. The rhythmic tap-tap-tap of his brush against the canvas was joined by the soft hum of voices, a symphony of learning and creation that filled the village air. He saw his students' growth, their pride in their accomplishments, and felt a deep sense of satisfaction. It was more than just teaching; it was a testament to his connection to the community, a way to ensure the legacy of his heritage lived on.

Beyond the temple and the art classes, he found himself deeply involved in the village's social fabric. He participated in the harvest festivals, his laughter blending with the joyful cries of the villagers as they celebrated the bounty of the land. He helped the elderly with their chores, offering a hand to those who needed it most. He sat by the ailing, offering a listening ear and a comforting presence. His empathy, once a dormant emotion buried beneath the layers of city stress, blossomed into a powerful force, shaping his interactions and enriching his life.

One evening, under the soft glow of the setting sun, he sat with the village elder, a woman named Amma, her face etched with the wisdom of a lifetime. They spoke of life, of loss, of acceptance, and of the profound beauty of simple existence. Amma spoke of the interconnectedness of all things, of how each individual's contribution, no matter how small, contributed to the overall harmony of the village. She spoke of finding peace not in chasing ambitious goals, but in appreciating the present moment, in embracing the rhythm of nature, and in serving one's community. Her words resonated deeply with him.

He understood then that his journey hadn't been about escaping the city; it had been about finding himself. The city had taught him ambition, the relentless pursuit of success. The village, in its quiet way, was teaching him humility, the importance of community, the profound joy of simple acts of service. He had traded the relentless pace of urban life for the gentle rhythm of the village, the constant pressure for a comforting sense of belonging.

He found himself falling in love again. Not a whirlwind romance of stolen glances and late-night whispers, but a quiet, gentle unfolding of affection. It started with shared smiles across the courtyard, a helping hand during the festivals, and quiet conversations under the starlit sky. She was a village girl, strong and independent, with a heart as warm and generous as the summer sun. She understood him, his past struggles, his quiet triumphs. She saw the depth of his spirit, the beauty of his soul, beyond the shadows of his urban past. Their love was a reflection of the village itself - peaceful, supportive, rooted in shared values. It was a love that nurtured his soul, healing the wounds of his past and nourishing his heart.

He began to understand the true meaning of home. It wasn't just a place; it was a feeling, a sense of belonging, a connection to something larger than himself. It was the familiar scent of incense burning in the temple, the warmth of his family's embrace, the friendly greetings of his neighbors, the quiet contentment of a life lived in harmony with nature and community. One day, a group of city dwellers, urban planners and tourists, arrived in the village. They were there to study the village's unique sustainable practices. Kumar, now a respected member of the community, acted as their guide, showcasing the village's self-sufficiency, its strong social fabric, and its harmonious relationship with the environment. He spoke passionately about the village's way of life, explaining how it had nurtured his spirit and brought him peace. He showed them his art, the murals that adorned the temple walls, the portraits that captured the essence of his neighbours. He told them his story. His tale of disillusionment and subsequent healing resonated deeply with some of the visitors, highlighting a counter-narrative to the allure of city life.

His story became a subtle testament to the restorative power of simple living. He became an advocate for the preservation of his community's way of life, protecting it from the encroaching influences of modernization. His art was not just a form of personal expression but a powerful tool for community advocacy, representing the very soul of his village. He found himself creating even more murals that captured the village's essence, the resilience of its people, and the importance of protecting its heritage. His paintings became symbols of hope and preservation, inspiring many to appreciate the beauty and significance of rural life.

As the years passed, Kumar's life settled into a rhythm that mirrored the gentle flow of the river that snaked through the village. His days were filled with meaningful work, his evenings with quiet moments of reflection. He found joy in the simple things, the taste of freshly harvested mangoes, the laughter of children playing in the fields, the comforting presence of his family and his beloved. He learned to cherish the small moments, the quiet celebrations, the shared joys and sorrows of a community that had embraced him as one of their own.

He had arrived in the village a broken man, burdened by the weight of unfulfilled ambitions, lost in the anonymity of the city. He left, years later, a whole man, his heart filled with a quiet contentment, his spirit nurtured by the embrace of his community. He had found acceptance, not just from the village, but from himself. The peace he found wasn't a mere absence of conflict; it was a positive state of being, a deep sense of belonging, purpose, and fulfillment. His journey was a testament to the transformative power of finding one's place, of embracing one's roots, and of allowing oneself to heal. His story, whispered through the generations, became a testament to the enduring strength of the human spirit and the enduring beauty of a life lived simply, authentically, and with purpose. The village, once a temporary refuge, had become his true home. He had found his peace.

Chapter 4

"The Soil Remembers"

"धरती पर जो बोया जाता है, वही लौटकर आता है – चाहे बीज हो या भावना।"

-Dushyant Kumar

(What you sow in the soil returns, be it a seed or a feeling.)

The city, a concrete jungle pulsating with a million heartbeats, a cacophony of honking vehicles and relentless activity, felt a world away now. It was a place of sharp angles and towering structures, a stark contrast to the gentle curves of the hills surrounding his village. The air, once thick with the smog of industry and exhaust fumes, now carried the sweet scent of wildflowers and damp earth. He remembered the suffocating anonymity of the city, the feeling of being lost in a sea of faces, a mere speck in a vast, indifferent metropolis. Here, in the village, he was known, he was valued, he was part of a community that embraced him as its own.

The relentless pressure to succeed, to climb the corporate ladder, to acquire material possessions – it all seemed so trivial now, so empty. In the city, success was measured in dollars and cents, promotions and prestige. He remembered the long hours, the late nights spent hunched over his computer screen, the constant gnawing anxiety that never seemed to leave him. He'd chased a phantom of happiness, a mirage of fulfillment, only to find himself perpetually unsatisfied, a victim of his own ambition.

The village, in contrast, offered a different kind of success – one measured not in material wealth, but in meaningful relationships, in acts of service, in the quiet satisfaction of a life lived in harmony with nature and community. He found himself valuing the simple pleasures – the warmth of the sun on his face, the gentle breeze rustling through the trees, the laughter of children at play. In the city, he had been surrounded by people, yet profoundly alone. In the village, he felt a profound sense of connection, a belonging that transcended the superficial relationships of the urban landscape.

The city had been a whirlwind of activity, a relentless chase, a relentless striving. Days bled into nights, blurring into a relentless pursuit of an elusive goal. He remembered the hurried meals, the snatched moments of rest, the constant pressure to perform, to achieve, to excel. The pace was frenetic, exhausting, and ultimately, unsatisfying. It left him feeling depleted, emotionally drained, a shell of his former self.

The village, on the other hand, moved at a different pace, a slower, gentler rhythm that mirrored the flow of the river and the changing seasons. There was time for reflection, time for contemplation, time for connection. The days unfolded organically, each moment unfolding naturally, without the relentless pressure of deadlines and appointments. There was a sense of peace, a tranquility that was completely absent from the chaotic energy of the city.

The emotional landscape was just as different. The city was a place of fierce competition, of cutthroat ambition, of relentless self-promotion. He remembered the constant jostling for position, the backstabbing, the betrayals, the feeling of being perpetually on edge. The city had eroded his trust, his empathy, his faith in humanity. He'd become cynical, hardened, wary of others' motives.

In the village, however, there was a sense of trust, of community, of shared values. He witnessed kindness, generosity, and mutual support in ways that were unimaginable in the city. People helped each other, shared their resources, and celebrated each other's successes. There was a collective spirit, a sense of unity that was remarkably comforting. He felt a sense of belonging, of being accepted for who he was, not for what he achieved.

The physical contrast was equally striking. The city was a concrete labyrinth, a maze of towering buildings and endless streets. Everything was artificial, manufactured, detached from the natural world. He remembered the lack of green spaces, the absence of fresh air, the oppressive weight of the urban environment.

The village, in contrast, was surrounded by nature. The landscape was alive, vibrant, filled with the sights and sounds of the natural world. He could breathe deeply, filling his lungs with fresh, clean air. The colours were more intense, the sounds more natural, the smells more earthy and fragrant. The village was a living, breathing organism, intimately connected to the rhythms of the earth. He found a solace in this connection, a sense of grounding that he had never experienced in the city.

Even the social interactions differed wildly. In the city, interactions were often superficial, fleeting, transactional. People were preoccupied with their own lives, their own ambitions, their own problems. There was little time for genuine connection, for meaningful conversation, for deep friendships.

In the village, however, relationships were deep, meaningful, long-lasting. He formed bonds with people that went beyond mere acquaintanceship. He shared laughter, tears, and experiences with his neighbours, friends, and family. The social fabric of the village was strong, resilient, and supportive. It provided a sense of security, a sense of belonging, a sense of community that he had never found in the anonymity of the city.

The quiet evenings in the village, spent under the starlit sky, offered a stark contrast to the noisy nights of the city. The constant hum of traffic, the blaring sirens, the relentless noise of urban life – all of that felt like a distant memory now. Here, the only sounds were the chirping of crickets, the rustling of leaves, and the gentle murmur of the river. It was a peaceful, restful existence, a haven from the constant stimulation of the city

His love for the village girl, a love that blossomed slowly and steadily, like a flower unfolding in the spring sun, further cemented his newfound peace. The city had taught him to pursue fleeting passions, to chase the next thrill, the next conquest. Here, in the village, he had learned the value of patience, of commitment, of genuine connection. Their relationship was rooted in mutual respect, shared values, and a deep understanding that transcended the superficiality of urban romance.

His transition from the city to the village was not just a geographical move; it was a profound transformation of his inner self. He shed the burdens of ambition, the anxieties of urban life, and the cynicism that had enveloped him. He found himself again, a stronger, more compassionate, more authentic version of himself. He had exchanged the frantic energy of the city for the gentle rhythm of the village, the relentless pursuit of success for the quiet contentment of a life lived simply and meaningfully. His journey was a testament to the restorative power of nature, the importance of community, and the profound beauty of a life lived authentically, in harmony with himself and the world around him. The city had been a chapter, a necessary but painful experience in his life's journey; the village, however, was his home, his sanctuary, the place where he finally found his peace.

The city lights, once a beacon of opportunity, now seemed like distant, flickering stars. They'd promised everything – success, wealth, recognition – but delivered only a gnawing emptiness. Kumar remembered the relentless grind, the suffocating pressure to conform, to compete, to excel. He'd envisioned a life of towering achievements, a career that would leave an indelible mark on the world. The reality, however, had been far less glamorous. It was a daily struggle for survival, a constant battle against the tide of ambition, a relentless pursuit of a goal that constantly shifted and morphed, always just out of reach.

He'd sacrificed so much for this elusive dream. His family, his friends, his sense of self – all had been relegated to the sidelines as he clawed his way up the corporate ladder. He'd sacrificed precious moments of connection for fleeting moments of professional validation. He traded intimate conversations for tense conference calls. The nights were filled with the hum of his laptop, the glow of the computer screen mirroring the ever-present anxieties that burrowed deep into his soul. Sleep became a luxury, a brief respite from the relentless pressure.

The irony wasn't lost on him. He'd envisioned the city as a place of freedom, a space where he could break free from the constraints of his village life, where he could forge his own path, where he could become the architect of his own destiny. Instead, he found himself trapped in a gilded cage of expectations, a prisoner of his own ambition. The freedom he'd sought had eluded him, replaced by a suffocating sense of confinement. The more he achieved, the more empty he felt. The accolades were hollow, the promotions meaningless, the wealth insignificant. They couldn't fill the void that had

opened up inside him. The city, once a symbol of progress and opportunity, had become a symbol of his failure, a monument to his unrealized dreams.

He thought of Chitra, the girl from his village, her face a canvas of serene beauty, her smile a beacon in the darkness of his city life. He'd pushed her away, convinced that his ambition demanded sacrifice, that his love for her was an obstacle in his path to success. He'd believed that the city, with its endless possibilities, was his only path to happiness. Now, he realised the profound error of his judgment. He'd traded true love for the fleeting glitter of professional success, and the exchange had left him profoundly impoverished.

The city had warped his perceptions, twisted his priorities, and eroded his values. He'd become consumed by the relentless pursuit of material success, measuring his worth by the size of his bank account, the title on his business card, and the envy of his colleagues. He'd lost sight of what truly mattered – genuine human connections, authentic relationships, and a life lived in harmony with his values. He'd become a stranger to himself, a shadow of the man he once was.

The return to the village had been a homecoming, not just to a physical place, but to himself. The scent of the earth, the warmth of the sun, the laughter of children – these simple pleasures had a profound effect on him. The village, with its slow pace of life and strong sense of community, offered a balm to his wounded soul. He found solace in the rhythmic pulse of life, the gentle ebb and flow of existence. The city's relentless pace had eroded his spirit, but here, he felt himself slowly healing, regenerating, reconnecting with the essential parts of himself that had been lost.

The people of the village, his neighbours, his friends, embraced him with open arms. They didn't judge him for his failures or his ambitions. They saw past his past mistakes, recognizing the essential goodness within him. They offered him acceptance, understanding, and unconditional love, a stark contrast to the competitive, often cutthroat environment of the city. He felt a profound sense of belonging, a connection to something larger than himself.

Kumar realised that his ambition had been misdirected. He'd sought external validation instead of internal peace. He'd chased fleeting success instead of lasting happiness. He'd defined himself by his accomplishments instead of his intrinsic worth. His journey had been a painful, yet necessary lesson in the importance of authenticity and self-acceptance.

He began to understand the subtle nuances of success that the city had failed to teach him. He'd equated success with material wealth and professional achievement, ignoring the quieter, more profound aspects of a successful life – strong relationships, inner peace, and a sense of purpose. He'd learned that true success wasn't measured in dollars and cents, but in the quality of his relationships, his contribution to his community, and the joy he found in everyday life.

The village, in its quiet simplicity, offered a different perspective. Success was not a singular, monumental achievement, but a series of small victories, a journey of personal growth, a testament to resilience, love and connection. It was about building meaningful relationships, supporting his community, and living in harmony with his environment. It was about finding contentment in the simple pleasures of life – the warmth of the sun, the taste of freshly picked mangoes, the laughter of children playing in the fields. The contrast between his urban and rural experiences served as a powerful reminder that success is not a destination but a journey, and that the pursuit of material wealth should never come at the expense of genuine human connections and inner peace. The city had taught him a valuable lesson, a painful but necessary lesson, and he carried it with him, a mark of his personal evolution. The village, however, was where he found his true north, his sense of direction, his peace, and finally, his love, not just in Chitra's embrace but in the embrace of a life he'd finally learned to live authentically. He was no longer chasing an elusive mirage; he was finally home.

The quiet evenings, filled with the sounds of nature and the comforting presence of Chitra, were far more fulfilling than the noisy nights spent amidst the frantic energy of the city. He'd finally found the success he'd been striving for, not in the towering skyscrapers of the urban landscape, but in the gentle embrace of his village, in the simplicity of life lived amidst the rustling leaves and the murmur of the river, a life built on love, connection, and a deep sense of belonging. He realised that his true ambition wasn't to conquer the world, but to find his place in it, to contribute to his community, and to live a life that was true to himself. The city had been a harsh teacher, but the lessons he'd learned had led him to a far richer, more fulfilling life than he could have ever imagined. The concrete jungle had given way to a verdant paradise, where his heart had finally found its home. And in that, he found his true success.

The journey had been arduous, filled with doubts, setbacks, and moments of profound despair. But it was also a journey of self-discovery, of personal growth, and of transformation. He'd learned to value the simple things, to appreciate the beauty of nature, and to cherish the people in his life. He'd shed the burden of his unrealistic ambitions, replaced them with realistic aspirations that aligned with his values and his heart's desires.

His reflection on his ambition and the realities of city life wasn't merely a recounting of events, but a profound exploration of his inner self, a journey into the heart of his being. It was a testament to the resilience of the human spirit, the capacity for change, and the enduring power of love and self-discovery. He was no longer defined by his past failures, but by his present contentment and the promise of a future built on authenticity, connection, and peace. The city had been a testing ground, a crucible where his spirit had been forged in the fires of ambition and adversity. But it was in the quiet tranquility of the village that he found his true self, a self that was stronger, wiser, and more complete than the ambitious young man who had set out to conquer the world. His journey had been a long and winding road, but it had ultimately led him home, to a place of peace, contentment, and lasting love. His ambition may have been misdirected, but his heart had found its true north, and in that, he found a success beyond measure.

The scent of woodsmoke and damp earth clung to him, a stark contrast to the sterile, artificial fragrance of the city's air fresheners. He sat on the worn wooden porch of his family's home, the rhythmic chirping of crickets a soothing balm to his frayed nerves. Chitra sat beside him, her hand resting lightly on his, her presence a silent reassurance. The city had been a whirlwind, a relentless maelstrom of ambition and disappointment, but here, in the quiet embrace of his village, he felt a sense of peace he hadn't known was possible.

He thought about Chitra, about the way she'd looked at him that last time he saw her before leaving for the city - a mixture of hope and apprehension mirroring his own conflicting emotions. He'd promised her a future filled with riches and success, a life beyond their wildest dreams. He'd painted vivid pictures of a life where they'd share a sprawling mansion, filled with laughter and luxury. He'd spoken of cars and clothes, of grand celebrations and holidays in exotic lands, everything he thought she deserved. But those promises had been hollow, born out of his ambition and fueled by the city's seductive whispers of prosperity.

He'd believed, in the heady early days of his career, that his success would be a testament to their love. He envisioned returning to the village, triumphant and wealthy, ready to sweep her off her feet and prove to her that his sacrifice had been worth it. He hadn't imagined the emptiness, the corrosive loneliness that would accompany his climb. He'd mistaken the city's glitter for gold, its fleeting pleasures for lasting happiness. His ascent had been a lonely one, devoid of the warmth and intimacy that Chitra offered.

The guilt gnawed at him. He'd traded her unwavering love for the uncertain promise of urban success. He'd chosen the thrill of the chase over the comfort of her embrace. He had convinced himself that distance would strengthen their bond, that the sacrifices he was making would ultimately benefit them both. The truth, however, was far more painful: distance had weakened their bond, and his sacrifices had only served to isolate him, both emotionally and physically.

He remembered their last conversation, a strained, fragmented dialogue across a vast expanse of miles. He'd spoken of deadlines and promotions, of meetings and presentations, his voice distant and preoccupied. He'd barely registered her words, her quiet concerns about his health, his well-being, his happiness. He had been so consumed by his own ambitions, so blinded by his desire for success, that he had failed to see the distress in her voice, the growing desperation in her eyes.

The betrayal wasn't a single, dramatic event, but a slow, insidious erosion of trust, a gradual dismantling of their connection. It was a series of missed calls, unanswered texts, postponed visits, and hastily scribbled emails. It was the slow drip, drip, drip of neglect that finally drowned their relationship. He hadn't intended to hurt her; he'd convinced himself that he was doing it for both of them, that his success would ultimately secure their happiness.

He'd rationalized his choices, telling himself that he was building a better future for them, a life that would exceed all their expectations. But in his relentless pursuit of success, he'd lost sight of the very thing that had made his life worth living: her love. He had become a stranger to himself, a shadow of the man he once was, a man who valued ambition over love, the material over the spiritual.

The city, with its relentless pace and cutthroat competition, had fostered a sense of detachment, an emotional coldness that had chilled his relationship with Chitra to its core. He had been so focused on achieving his goals that he'd neglected the most important relationship in his life. He'd measured his success in monetary terms, forgetting that true success is measured in the richness of human connection.

Now, back in the village, surrounded by the quiet beauty of nature and the unwavering support of his community, he saw the magnitude of his error. The city had offered him a facade of success, a mirage of happiness, but it was in the simplicity of village life that he found true contentment. He saw now that his ambition had been misdirected, that he'd mistaken the glittering surface of success for its true essence.

Chitra's love had been a constant, a steady beacon in the stormy seas of his ambition. But he'd ignored it, dismissed it, believing that it was an obstacle in his path to success. The irony was crushing. He'd sought success in the city, only to find that he'd lost the very thing that gave his life meaning. He'd traded real love for a fleeting illusion. He'd chased a dream, a mirage of success, only to wake up to the bitter realization that he'd lost everything of true value.

The villagers, with their quiet understanding and acceptance, had helped him to see his past mistakes with clarity and compassion. They hadn't judged him, but had offered him a space to heal, a place to reconnect with himself and with Chitra. Their unwavering support had been a crucial element in his journey of self-discovery. He realized he'd sought external validation instead of internal peace, and now he could start seeking the latter.

The reconciliation wasn't easy. There were tears, apologies, and long, heartfelt conversations. There was a deep sense of regret, of lost time, of opportunities squandered. But there was also a profound sense of forgiveness, a mutual understanding, and a renewed commitment to build a life together, a life based not on the fleeting promise of material success, but on the enduring strength of their love.

He realized that love isn't a destination, but a journey, a continuous process of growth, understanding, and forgiveness. It requires nurturing, patience, and a willingness to compromise. He'd learned a harsh lesson, a lesson etched in the loneliness of the city and the quiet acceptance of the village. The city had taught him the limits of ambition, and the village had shown him the true value of love and belonging. He held Chitra's hand tighter, the touch grounding him in the present moment, erasing the ghosts of his past failures.

He knew his journey of self-discovery was far from over. He had much to learn, much to overcome. But he was no longer alone. He had Chitra, his village, and a newfound understanding of himself. He was rebuilding his life, brick by brick, based on authenticity, connection, and the unwavering support of the people who loved him. The city lights, once a symbol of his ambition, now held no allure. His true home, his true success, was here, in the quiet embrace of his village, in the unwavering love of Chitra, and in the peace he had finally found within himself. The city had been a detour, a painful but necessary lesson, leading him ultimately to a far more profound and fulfilling destination: a life lived authentically, in harmony with his heart, and with the love of his life by his side. The journey had been difficult, but the rewards were immeasurable, a testament to the enduring power of love and the resilience of the human spirit.

The dust of the city still clung to him, a gritty residue on his clothes, his skin, even in his soul. But the air here, in his village, felt different – cleaner, sharper, carrying the scent of familiar earth and the distant smoke of cooking fires. He sat with Chitra, her hand clasped firmly in his, the silence between them comfortable, a testament to the unspoken understanding that had finally blossomed. The city, that glittering behemoth of ambition and broken dreams, had taught him lessons far harsher than any textbook ever could. He had chased success with a ferocity that bordered on obsession, believing that material wealth would fill the emptiness he carried within. He'd envisioned a life of luxury, a life beyond the simple existence of his village, a life he believed Chitra deserved. He'd pictured himself, a triumphant victor, returning to sweep her off her feet with the spoils of his urban conquest. The reality, however, was a stark and brutal awakening. The city, despite its dazzling facade, had proven to be a lonely place, a landscape populated by ambitious strangers vying for the same fleeting rewards.

The cutthroat competition, the relentless pressure to succeed, had eroded his sense of self. He'd become a stranger to himself, sacrificing his emotional well-being at the altar of ambition. He'd measured his success in terms of his bank balance, neglecting the far richer currency of human connection. He'd been so focused on the climb that he'd missed the breathtaking view, the simple joys that truly mattered. He'd chased shadows, believing they were substance.

One of the most poignant lessons he'd learned was the ephemeral nature of superficial success. The city's glittering lights, the sleek cars, the opulent apartments – they were all temporary, fleeting symbols of a success that felt hollow and unsatisfying. He'd traded genuine contentment for a gilded cage, a life devoid of warmth, love, and genuine connection. He'd thought wealth would bring happiness, but it only amplified his loneliness, a cruel irony he couldn't ignore.

The city had also revealed the fragility of his own identity. Away from the familiar comfort of his village, away from the grounding presence of his family and friends, he'd felt lost, adrift in a sea of unfamiliar faces and competing ambitions. He'd tried to define himself through his achievements, through the accolades he received, through the accumulation of material possessions. He'd learned that true identity isn't found in external validation but in the quiet understanding of one's own inner self.

The experience had forced him to confront his own shortcomings, his own vulnerabilities. He'd been driven by a fear of failure, a fear of not living up to the expectations he'd set for himself. He'd allowed this fear to dictate his choices, to cloud his judgment, to drive him away from the things that truly mattered. The city, in its relentless pursuit of productivity, had amplified that fear until it was a constant companion, a whispering shadow that consumed him.

He'd also learned the immeasurable value of forgiveness. Forgiveness of himself, for the mistakes he'd made, for the hurt he'd caused, and forgiveness of Chitra, for the time he'd wasted and the pain he'd inflicted. The path to reconciliation hadn't been easy; it required honesty, humility, and a willingness to confront the past without judgment or self-pity. The process was cathartic, a shedding of the old self to make way for a new, more authentic version.

The village, in contrast to the city's frenetic energy, had offered a sanctuary, a place to heal and reconnect. The quiet rhythm of village life, the unwavering support of his community, had helped him rediscover his roots, his identity, and his sense of belonging. It was a stark contrast to the isolation he had experienced in the city, a stark reminder that true strength doesn't lie in individual achievement but in shared experiences, mutual support, and community.

The villagers, with their quiet dignity and resilience, had taught him the importance of empathy, compassion, and understanding. They hadn't judged his failures but had embraced him with open arms, reminding him that mistakes were a part of life, a necessary ingredient in the process of growth and self-discovery. This acceptance had allowed him to embrace his mistakes, to learn from them, and to move forward without the weight of guilt or shame.

His relationship with Chitra had been the cornerstone of this journey of self-discovery. Their reconciliation had been a testament to the enduring power of love, its ability to withstand the trials and tribulations of life, to heal wounds, and to rebuild shattered connections. He realized that love wasn't a passive state of being; it demanded continuous effort, understanding, and a willingness to compromise. He had failed in those areas, but their reconciliation had given him the strength to rectify his mistakes and nurture a love that ran deeper and more profoundly than he'd ever imagined.

He had learned that true success isn't defined by material possessions or societal accolades. It's measured in the richness of human connection, in the warmth of love and belonging, in the quiet contentment of a life lived authentically. The city had been a harsh but invaluable teacher, a crucible that had forged him into a stronger, more compassionate, and more self-aware individual.

The lessons he'd learned in the city were not merely personal; they were universal truths applicable to anyone who chases ambition, who seeks fulfillment in external validations instead of inner peace. The experience had gifted him a perspective that extended beyond his own personal narrative, allowing him to empathize with others who had also ventured down the path of misplaced ambition, who had chased the chimera of success at the cost of their emotional well-being.

He looked at Chitra, her eyes reflecting the warm glow of the setting sun. Her hand in his felt secure, solid, grounding. The city had taught him the limits of ambition, and the village had shown him the immeasurable value of love and belonging. He'd traded a fleeting illusion for a genuine reality, a life rich in meaning and authentic connection. He'd arrived at a place of true success, a place of acceptance, a place of love – a place far more valuable than any glittering city could ever offer. The journey had been painful, yes, but the rewards were infinitely greater, exceeding all expectations. He was home. He was whole. He was happy. And that, he realized, was the greatest success of all.

The scent of jasmine and woodsmoke hung heavy in the air, a familiar perfume that soothed the anxieties that had plagued him for so long in the city. He inhaled deeply, the earthy fragrance grounding him in a way the sterile air of his city apartment never could. Here, surrounded by the gentle rhythm of village life, the constant hum of urban chaos faded into a distant, almost unreal memory. The city, with its relentless pursuit of achievement and its cold indifference to the human spirit, felt like a bad dream now, a harsh lesson learned and left behind.

Chitra sat beside him, her presence a silent comfort, a warm hearth in the quiet twilight. He traced the lines on her palm, each crease a map of their shared journey, a testament to the love that had weathered the storm of his ambition. Their silence was not an emptiness but a space filled with unspoken understanding, a profound connection forged in the crucible of his self-imposed exile and subsequent return.

He had returned to the village a changed man, stripped bare of the illusions he'd clung to so fiercely in the city. The veneer of success he'd painstakingly constructed had crumbled, revealing the insecure and vulnerable man beneath. The realization had been painful, a slow, agonizing shedding of a false identity. But within that pain, a profound sense of freedom emerged. He had finally begun to understand himself, to accept his imperfections, and to embrace the complexities of his own being.

The city had taught him the value of humility. He'd arrived with a swagger, convinced of his own superiority, blinded by the self-importance that urban life seemed to breed. He had believed himself to be better, more accomplished, more deserving than those who remained in the village. This arrogance had been his undoing, a fatal flaw that had poisoned his relationships and his sense of self. The city's relentless pursuit of status and recognition had only amplified this arrogance, creating a chasm between him and the very people he cared for most.

Returning home, he saw the village with new eyes. He noticed the intricate patterns in the mud walls, the artistry in the simple woven mats, the silent dignity in the weathered faces of his elders. He listened to their stories, stories of resilience, of survival, of quiet joys found in simple things. He realized that success didn't reside in towering skyscrapers or overflowing bank accounts but in the quiet contentment of a life lived in harmony with oneself and one's community. The city had shown him the superficiality of external validation; the village showed him the true depth of inner peace.

His relationship with Chitra had undergone a profound transformation. He'd returned not as the conquering hero he'd envisioned, but as a man humbled by his mistakes, seeking forgiveness and understanding. Chitra, in her wisdom and grace, had met him halfway, her love a beacon guiding him through the darkness of his self-doubt. Their reconciliation had been a testament to the resilience of their bond, a proof of the power of love to heal even the deepest wounds.

The forgiveness he sought wasn't merely from Chitra; it was also from himself. He'd spent so long judging his own shortcomings, berating himself for his failures, that he'd lost sight of his own inherent worth. He had to learn to forgive himself for the choices he'd made, the opportunities he'd missed, the hurts he'd inflicted. This process of self-forgiveness was the most arduous part of his journey, but also the most liberating

He spent hours sitting by the river, watching the water flow, a constant reminder of the impermanence of things. The city's relentless pursuit of permanence, of accumulating possessions, of building a lasting legacy, seemed foolish in the face of nature's cyclical rhythms. He learned to appreciate the beauty of impermanence, to see the value in the fleeting moments, in the changing seasons, in the ephemeral beauty of a sunset.

The village offered him a different kind of education, one that wasn't found in textbooks or boardrooms. He learned about community, about shared responsibility, about mutual support. He witnessed the intricate network of relationships that bound the villagers together, a tapestry of interdependence that fostered a sense of belonging he'd never experienced in the city. The city had emphasized individuality; the village highlighted the strength of collectivity.

He found solace in the simple rituals of village life, in the shared meals, in the festivals, in the quiet evenings spent with his family and friends. These simple acts, which he'd once dismissed as mundane, now held a profound significance, a reminder of the deep-seated human need for connection and belonging. He participated in village life fully, finding satisfaction in his contribution to the community. The sense of purpose he discovered here surpassed anything he'd ever achieved in the city. He realized that true success wasn't about achieving a certain level of wealth or status, but about living a life aligned with his values, a life grounded in authenticity and integrity. He'd traded the glittering façade of the city for the genuine richness of his village life, a choice he'd never regret. The city had taught him the harsh realities of ambition; the village had shown him the beauty of simplicity.

The scars of his past remained, reminders of the lessons he'd learned. But they were no longer wounds that festered and bled; they were marks of a journey, testaments to his growth and resilience. He carried them with him, not as burdens but as badges of honor, symbols of his transformation from a lost soul in a concrete jungle to a grounded individual finding peace and purpose in the heart of his village.

He sat with Chitra, her hand resting gently on his, and watched the stars emerge in the darkening sky. The city, with its artificial lights, could never reproduce the ethereal beauty of this night, this quietude, this profound sense of homecoming. He had found his true self, not in the pursuit of fleeting ambition, but in the embrace of love, community, and the quiet wisdom of his village. His journey had been long and arduous, but he had arrived, finally, at a place of peace, a place of belonging, a place of home. And in that homecoming, he found true and lasting success.

A Letter Never Sent

(Found folded between the pages of an old city notebook)

Dear Chitra,

Pata nahin tum yeh kabhi padho gi ya nahin. Shayad main yeh tumhare liye likh raha hoon, ya shayad apne uss khoye hue khud ke liye. Ya phir bas tumhari rooh ki kami mehsoos karne ke liye,chahe sirf in alfaazon ke zariye hi sahi.

Ajeeb hai na, kaise khamoshi waqt ke saath aur tez ho jaati hai. Kaise jo baatein maine tumse kabhi nahi kahi, woh shehar ki har shor se zyada goonj uthi hai mere zehen mein.

Maine tumhe kaha tha ki main jaa raha hoon tumhare liye ek bright future banane , bade ghar, mehenga khana, khubsoorat saree. Par maine yeh nahi bataya ki main kitna dar gaya tha. Shehar se nahi, khud se. Mushkilaat se. Apni waadon pe khara na utarne se.

Raaton ko baar-baar tumhare baare mein socha. Tumhari muskaan, tumhari hansee, waisa hi tarika jab tum ghabra jaati ho, jab apne choodi ko kheench leti ho,sab kuch mere saath boardrooms mein, lifts mein, akeli cab rides mein mere peechhe bhaagta raha.

Main khud ko yaqeen dilata raha ki yeh doori temporary hai. Ek din main wapas aaunga, jeet ke, laayak ban ke. Par sach yeh hai,jitna zyada main chadha, utna zyada main khud ko gawa baitha. Wahi jo kabhi mera ghar thi,*tum*.

Shehar ki shor se zyada main tumhari khamoshi ko miss kiya. Tumhari aankhon ko miss kiya, jo kabhi bolne se pehle hi sab kuch keh jaati thi. *Humen* miss kiya. Woh "hum" jo main kabhi sochta tha ki badal jayega, par woh pehle se hi khoobsurat tha , usi main main khoya raha.

Call karna chahiye tha. Wapas aana chahiye tha. Tumhe jhappi deke kehna chahiye tha, "Tum hi kafi ho. Yeh gaon kafi hai. *Hum* kafi hain."

Par maine nahi kiya.

Ab bas yeh letter baaki hai.

Shayad ek din mere paas himmat hogi yeh tum tak pohchane ki. Ya shayad yeh hamesha ke liye sangrahit rahega, jaise humari zindagi bhi,khamosh, khubsurat, aur lagbhag kho gayi.

Mujhe maaf kar do, agar ho sake.
Khamoshi ke liye. Dooriyon ke liye. Mayaari safalta ki peeche bhagte hue tumhare intezaar ke liye.

Hamesha tumhara,
Kumar

Chapter 5:

"The Third Man Speaks"

"मैं अकेला ही चला था जानिब-ए-मंज़िल मगर,

लोग साथ आते गए और कारवाँ बनता गया।"

-Majrooh Sultanpuri

(I had started alone toward my destination, but people kept joining me, and a caravan formed.)

The morning mist still clung to the rice paddies as Kumar rose, the faint chirping of crickets a gentle alarm clock. The city's jarring cacophony of horns and sirens felt like a distant, bad dream. He moved through the familiar routines of his new life with a quiet grace, a stark contrast to the frenetic energy that had once defined him. His days no longer revolved around boardroom meetings and ambitious targets; now, they were measured in the rhythm of prayers, the warmth of community, and the quiet satisfaction of service. The small temple, nestled amongst the ancient banyan trees, was his sanctuary. The scent of incense and sandalwood filled the air, a comforting aroma that replaced the sterile, artificial perfumes of his city apartment. He swept the stone floor with meticulous care, his movements deliberate and peaceful. Each task, from polishing the brass lamps to arranging the marigold garlands, was a form of meditation, a connection to something larger than himself.

His days were filled with a quiet intensity. He spent hours studying ancient scriptures, the sacred texts revealing layers of meaning that had previously eluded him. He learned the intricate nuances of Sanskrit chanting, his voice resonating with a newfound depth and understanding. The city had taught him the power of words to manipulate and persuade; here, he learned the power of words to comfort, to inspire, to heal.

The villagers, once strangers, now felt like family. He knew their stories, their struggles, their joys. He offered solace to the grieving, guidance to the lost, and a listening ear to those burdened with worries. He learned the art of empathy, the importance of genuine connection, a skill he'd never cultivated in the competitive, individualistic world of urban life. The villagers, in their quiet generosity, welcomed him, offering him not pity, but respect. They saw in him not a fallen man, but a soul seeking redemption, and they embraced him as one of their own.

His interactions with the villagers were a constant source of learning and growth. He learned about their farming practices, their intricate system of water management, their deep connection to the land. He marveled at their resilience, their ability to find joy amidst hardship, their unwavering faith in the face of adversity. He witnessed the strength of their community, the way they supported each other, shared their resources, and celebrated their triumphs and mourned their losses together. It was a life far removed from the isolation and anonymity of the city. Evenings were spent sharing meals with the villagers, the simple fare a feast for his soul. He sat on woven mats, listening to their stories, their laughter echoing through the courtyard. He shared his own experiences, not as boasts of past achievements, but as lessons learned, mistakes made, and wisdom gained. His honesty was disarming, his vulnerability inspiring. He found a freedom in sharing his story, a release from the burden of his carefully constructed city persona.

His relationship with Chitra blossomed anew. Their love story wasn't a fairytale, but a testament to resilience and forgiveness. They spent their evenings side-by-side, their silence a comfortable companionship. He learned the value of quiet moments, of shared silences that held more depth than words could ever express. She supported his new path, understanding the profound transformation he had undergone. Their love wasn't about grand gestures or lavish displays of affection; it was a quiet, unwavering commitment, a steady flame that warmed their hearts and illuminated their lives.

One day, an elderly woman approached him, her eyes filled with tears. Her grandson, a young man who had migrated to the city in search of a better life, had fallen ill. She spoke of his loneliness, his desperation, the harsh realities of city life that had crushed his spirit. Kumar listened patiently, offering words of comfort and hope. He understood her pain; he had experienced the city's harsh indifference firsthand. He knew that he had to be more than just a priest in this context; he had to be an anchor, a point of hope for those who were suffering from the same struggles. He felt an obligation to act on that understanding.

He decided to use his past connections in the city to help. He started by contacting some old friends and acquaintances to see if he could get some assistance for the boy, and that's how he found a hospital that was willing to give the young man the medical care he needed. Although he had left his city life behind, he understood the importance of utilising his past networks and resources to serve his current community.

This act of service wasn't merely an act of compassion; it was a symbol of his transformation, a testament to his commitment to his new life. It was a reminder that his past experiences, though painful, had shaped him into a man capable of profound empathy and action. The city had taught him ambition; the village taught him compassion. The city had shown him the coldness of indifference; the village showed him the warmth of community. He found his true vocation not in the pursuit of personal gain, but in the service of others.

His journey was far from over. He knew that life would throw new challenges his way, but he faced them with a newfound confidence, a quiet strength born from his experiences and his deep-seated faith. He had found peace not in the pursuit of wealth or status, but in the simple act of service, in the quiet contentment of a life lived with purpose and integrity. The city's glittering facade had faded into the background, replaced by the gentle beauty of his village, the warmth of his community, and the unwavering love of Chitra. His transformation wasn't merely physical; it was spiritual, profound, and complete. He had found his true home, not in a place, but within himself, a home built on humility, compassion, and the unwavering pursuit of a life lived in service to others. The city had tried to define him, to shape him into a product of its relentless ambition; but the village had nurtured his soul, allowing him to blossom into the man he was always meant to be. And in that blossoming, he found true love, true fulfillment, and true peace. His past was not something to run from, but a stepping stone to the future he had always dreamed of, yet could only achieve by letting go of his old self.

The rhythmic thud of the dholak, the lilting melody of the bansuri, and the joyous shouts of children playing,these were the sounds that now composed

Kumar's evenings. Gone were the sterile silence of his city apartment, the incessant hum of traffic, and the echoing loneliness of his high-rise existence. He sat on a woven mat in the courtyard, surrounded by the villagers, sharing a simple meal of rice, dal, and vegetables. The food was delicious, of course, but the real feast was the conversation, the laughter, the shared stories.

Old Man Sharma, with his twinkling eyes and a mischievous grin, recounted tales of his youth, his adventures as a young shepherd boy, his escapades with his friends. His stories, seasoned with the spice of exaggeration and the warmth of fond memories, were a window into a past that resonated with the timeless simplicity of village life. He spoke of the monsoon season, of the land coming alive, of the rich harvest that followed. He spoke of community spirit, where everyone worked together for everyone's welfare, regardless of any differences. He spoke of the value of every single grain of rice that was produced.

Young Radha, her cheeks flushed with the heat of the fire, shared her anxieties about her upcoming marriage. Her concerns were simple but profound: the fear of leaving her family, the uncertainty of her new life, the longing for her mother's comforting presence. Kumar listened patiently, offering words of encouragement, assuring her of the enduring strength of family bonds, even across distances. He drew parallels between her apprehension and his own initial anxieties when he had first moved to the city, emphasizing the power of adaptation, of resilience. He spoke of the importance of preserving one's individuality even within a marriage.

Evenings were not just about stories and anxieties; they were filled with songs, mostly folksongs, each telling a story of love, loss, courage, and resilience,a living tapestry of the community's history and emotions. The women of the village, their voices harmonious, sang songs that spoke of the bounty of the earth, the cycle of life, and the unwavering strength of human spirit. Their melodies, simple yet moving, spoke of the interconnectedness of life, a web of relationships that bound them together. Kumar found it so beautiful that he learned a few of the songs, singing along with them, his voice blending seamlessly with the chorus of experienced voices. The songs weren't just songs; they were the vibrant beating heart of the community.

The men would often discuss the current affairs of the village: the upcoming harvest festival, the repair of the village well, the progress of the irrigation project. Kumar, initially an outsider, was now an active participant in these discussions. He offered his suggestions, his perspectives honed by his years in the city, but always tempered with respect for the wisdom of the elders. His suggestions were always met with an open mind, and he never failed to learn something new. His perspective was welcomed because he didn't patronize them with his past; he respected their views.

His relationship with Chitra deepened with each passing day. They walked together through the rice paddies, their footsteps leaving barely a trace on the soft earth. They sat together under the shade of the banyan trees, the rustling leaves a soothing symphony. They did not need words; their shared silence was a language richer than any spoken tongue. Their love was no longer a tempestuous storm but a gentle stream, flowing steadily, nourishing their souls, and connecting them to the heart of their community. Chitra's understanding of the transformation Kumar had undergone helped strengthen their bond. She celebrated his newfound purpose in life.

The villagers, once wary of this city-bred stranger, now treated him with affection and respect. They sought his advice on personal matters, shared their joys and sorrows, and included him in all aspects of community life. He was no longer Kumar, the ambitious executive; he was Kumar, the kind priest who helped his community grow. He attended village meetings, helped with religious festivals, participated in community projects, and offered emotional support to those in need.

One day, a young boy named Rohan approached Kumar, his eyes wide with fear. His pet goat, a small, white creature named Moti, had gone missing. Kumar, remembering his own childhood longing for his family's pets, immediately understood the boy's distress. He joined the search party, his city-bred efficiency surprising the villagers. He organized the search, dividing the group into smaller teams, assigning specific areas to each, and establishing a communication system. Their combined efforts successfully located the missing goat, bringing joy and relief to the boy and his family. This simple act of helping someone find their lost pet became a symbol of his integration into the community.

Another time, a severe storm caused widespread damage to the village's crops. Kumar, using his knowledge of the city's bureaucratic processes, assisted the villagers in securing government aid, navigating the complexities of paperwork and applications. He helped the villagers organize themselves and present a united front when it came to appealing for aid. The support of the whole community had proven to be effective in getting assistance. His expertise, once used to acquire profits for a company, was now used for the benefit of his community.

His past, the city's relentless ambition, the corporate cutthroat competition, now seemed distant, almost unreal. It was a life he had left behind, but not forgotten. The lessons he had learned, the experiences he had accumulated, shaped him into a man who understood both the harsh realities of city life and the quiet resilience of rural existence. He realized the importance of community ties, how it helps individuals grow and become better versions of themselves.

His new life wasn't just a change of location; it was a transformation of spirit. He had found his purpose, his calling, in the service of his community, in the quiet contentment of a life lived with integrity and purpose. The city had offered him ambition; the village offered him peace. The city had offered him isolation; the village offered him belonging. The city had offered him success; the village offered him fulfillment. The city had tested him; the village had nurtured him. He had found his home, his love, and his peace, not in the glittering spires of a metropolis, but in the humble embrace of a village community that had welcomed him as one of their own. His journey from the city to the village was not merely a geographical shift; it was a homecoming, a return to the essence of who he truly was. His past was a lesson learned, his present a testament to his strength, and his future, a promise of a life lived in love, service, and unwavering community bonds.

The morning sun, a gentle hand, awakened Kumar. He didn't jolt awake to the jarring shriek of an alarm clock, but to the chirping of birds, a symphony orchestrated by nature itself. He lay for a moment, savoring the quietude, the stillness that had become his constant companion. The city's relentless clamor, once his daily bread, was now a distant memory, a faded echo in the vast expanse of his peaceful existence. He rose, a sense of calm washing over him, a tranquility that stemmed not from the absence of activity, but from a deep, abiding sense of purpose.

He walked to the river, the cool water a balm to his skin. He watched the sun paint the sky with hues of orange and gold, a spectacle that held more beauty than any city skyline. The river flowed, a steady, unwavering rhythm, mirroring the peace that had settled in his heart. He dipped his hands in the water, feeling its cool touch. It was a symbol of purification, of washing away the dust and grime of his past, leaving him feeling cleansed, renewed.

His past, once a source of anxiety and uncertainty, had become a wellspring of wisdom. He no longer viewed it with regret, but with acceptance, a quiet understanding that every experience, good or bad, had shaped him into the man he was today. The ambition that had once consumed him, the relentless pursuit of success, no longer held the same allure. He had tasted that success, had reached the pinnacle of his career, and found it hollow, unsatisfying. The emptiness had driven him back to the source, back to the roots of his being.

The village had offered him not just a change of scenery but a change of heart. It had stripped away the layers of artifice, the masks he had worn in the city, revealing the essence of his soul, a soul yearning for authenticity, for connection, for purpose. He found himself spending hours contemplating the profound truths of life, his mind at peace, his spirit renewed. He understood that true success wasn't about climbing the corporate ladder, but about finding one's inner peace and making a meaningful contribution to the world.

He found solace in the simple rituals of village life, the daily grind that was interwoven with the fabric of the community. He helped Chitra with her chores, shared the burden of her household tasks, participating in the day-to-day activities that formed the backbone of village life. The shared work strengthened their bond, forging a deeper understanding and affection between them. His hands, once accustomed to the smooth surface of a computer keyboard, now felt the roughness of the earth, the texture of the paddy fields, the cool smoothness of the river stones. This physical connection to the land grounded him, rooted him in a way that his city life never had.

His relationship with Chitra had blossomed into something profound. It was no longer the whirlwind romance of the city, but a quiet, steady love that deepened with each passing day. Their shared laughter echoed in the tranquility of the evening, their shared silences filled with unspoken understanding. They had found a love that transcended the fleeting passions of youth, a love that was rooted in mutual respect, in shared values, in a deep connection to their community. Their love story was no longer a tale of two individuals but a tale of two souls intertwined with the heart of their village.

He sat under the banyan tree, its wide-spreading branches offering shade and comfort. He watched the children play, their carefree laughter filling the air, a reminder of his own innocent childhood days. He remembered the games he played with his siblings, the stories his grandmother told him, the simple joys of a life lived in close communion with nature and family. The memories, once distant and blurry, came to him with sharp clarity, no longer marred by regret or bitterness. The city had taken away his childhood, but the village had given it back to him, a renewed appreciation for his past, and a peace in his present.

His days were filled with a sense of purpose, a feeling of contribution that he had never experienced in the city. He assisted the village elders, offering his skills and knowledge whenever needed. He used his city-bred efficiency to organize community projects, his sharp mind to solve practical problems, his compassionate heart to soothe troubled souls. He taught the children, sharing his knowledge not just of academics, but of life, of values, of integrity. His life had become a tapestry woven from the threads of service, compassion, and understanding.

The nights brought a different kind of serenity. He would lie down on the roof of his house, gazing at the starlit sky, a vast expanse of cosmic wonder that mirrored the boundless possibilities of his life. He listened to the night sounds of the village: the rustling of leaves, the croaking of frogs, the distant bark of a dog – a symphony of nature's lullaby. The silence was not empty but filled with a sense of peace, a sense of completeness.

Kumar had found more than just peace; he had found himself. The city had challenged him, tested his limits, pushed him to the brink. The village had embraced him, nurtured him, allowed him to heal. He had shed the persona he had created in the city, the ambitious executive striving for recognition and success, and embraced the man he truly was, a man of integrity, a man of compassion, a man at peace with himself and the world. His journey had been one of transformation, a pilgrimage of the soul, a return to his roots, and ultimately, a discovery of his true home. His heart found solace in the gentle rhythm of the village, not in the relentless pursuit of his past life, finding peace and fulfillment he could have only dreamed of in the city. The transformation was not just external, but a profound inner peace that emanated from his renewed sense of purpose and belonging. His life had reached a harmonious equilibrium, his spirit at rest, his heart full of contentment. He had not merely found peace; he had found himself, in the simple beauty of village life, nestled within the hearts of a loving and welcoming community.

The scent of jasmine hung heavy in the air, a sweet perfume that mingled with the earthy aroma of freshly tilled soil. Kumar, his hands stained with the rich brown of the earth, paused in his work, a gentle smile playing on his lips. He was helping Chitra's family harvest their rice paddy, the rhythmic swish of the sickles a soothing counterpoint to the chirping of crickets hidden in the tall grass. The sun beat down, but the work was not arduous; it was a shared effort, a communal rhythm that bound the villagers together. And in the midst of this shared labor, he found a new kind of joy, a contentment that had eluded him in the frenetic pace of city life.

He glanced at Chitra, her dark eyes sparkling with laughter as she effortlessly bundled the stalks of rice. Her movements were fluid, graceful, a testament to years spent working the land. She had a natural beauty, a radiance that stemmed not from makeup or expensive clothes, but from a deep connection to her roots, to her community, to the land that sustained her. It was a beauty that resonated deep within Kumar, touching a part of him he hadn't known existed.

Their conversations, once stilted and hesitant, now flowed freely, effortlessly, like the river that snaked through the heart of the village. They spoke of everything and nothing – the weather, the harvest, the village gossip, the distant rumble of a thunderstorm gathering on the horizon. But beneath the surface of these simple conversations lay a deeper current, a silent understanding that transcended words.

One evening, as they walked along the riverbank, the setting sun painting the sky in vibrant hues of orange and purple, Chitra paused, her gaze fixed on the shimmering water. Kumar followed her gaze, feeling the gentle breeze ruffling his hair. The silence between them was comfortable, a shared space filled with unspoken feelings.

"The city…it must have been very different," Chitra said softly, her voice barely a whisper.

Kumar nodded, a wistful smile touching his lips. "It was…a different world. Fast-paced, always rushing, always striving. I never really had time to…breathe."

"Here," Chitra said, gesturing towards the tranquil landscape, "we have time. Time for everything. Time to work, time to laugh, time to simply be."

Kumar looked at her, truly looked at her, seeing beyond the simple beauty of her features, into the depths of her soul. He saw a kindness, a gentleness, a strength that was both humbling and inspiring. He saw a woman who was deeply rooted in her community, a woman who found joy in the simplest things, a woman who possessed an inner peace that he envied, and admired deeply. A woman he was finding himself drawn to in ways he hadn't anticipated.

Days turned into weeks, weeks into months. Their connection deepened, strengthened by shared experiences, shared laughter, shared silences. They worked side-by-side, their hands often brushing as they tended to the crops, their eyes meeting in brief, fleeting glances that spoke volumes. They shared meals with her family, the aroma of freshly cooked food filling the air, the sound of laughter and conversation weaving a tapestry of warmth and belonging.

Kumar found himself participating in village festivals, his city-bred reserve melting away under the infectious enthusiasm of the villagers. He learned to play the dhol, his clumsy attempts eliciting laughter and encouragement from Chitra and her friends. He even joined in the traditional dances, his stiff movements gradually becoming more fluid, more confident, reflecting the ease and grace that was seeping into every aspect of his life.
He discovered a hidden talent for pottery, his city-honed precision translating into intricately designed bowls and vases. Chitra was his enthusiastic supporter, her encouragement fueling his creativity. He sold his creations at the weekly

market, the small profit a testament to his newfound self-reliance and his integration into the village community.

The quiet evenings spent under the banyan tree, once filled with solitary contemplation, were now shared moments of intimacy, of whispered conversations and shared secrets. They would talk for hours, their voices barely audible above the chirping of crickets and the gentle rustling of leaves. They talked about their dreams, their fears, their hopes for the future. They talked about the past, about their experiences, the paths that had led them to this unexpected meeting point.

One starlit night, sitting close under the banyan tree, Chitra confessed her own apprehensions about his leaving. She spoke of her fear of losing the connection they had developed, the easy companionship, the unspoken understanding that had become the anchor of her days. "I never thought I'd find someone like you here," she admitted, her voice barely above a whisper. "Someone from the city, yet…so much a part of us."

Kumar reached out, taking her hand in his. Her skin was soft, warm, and the simple touch sent a wave of emotion through him. He looked into her eyes, seeing a depth of feeling that mirrored his own.

"And I never thought I'd find a peace like this," he replied, his voice thick with emotion. "A connection, a belonging, a love…I never knew existed."

Their relationship blossomed slowly, organically, like a delicate flower unfurling its petals in the warmth of the sun. It was not the whirlwind romance of the city, but a quiet, steady love that was rooted in shared values, shared experiences, and a deep connection to their community. It was a love that nourished the soul, a love that gave him a sense of belonging he had never known.

He helped Chitra with her family's chores, sharing the burden of her household tasks. He learned the nuances of village life, participating in the daily grind that was interwoven with the fabric of the community. He helped the village elders, offering his skills and knowledge whenever needed, his compassion touching the hearts of the villagers. He shared his knowledge with the children, teaching them not just academics, but the values of life, of integrity, of compassion.

The city, once his ambition, his identity, his whole world, had become a distant memory. His past, once a source of anxiety and uncertainty, had become a wellspring of wisdom. He had found his purpose, not in the relentless pursuit of success, but in the quiet joy of simple living, in the profound connection to a community that had welcomed him with open arms.

His life in the village was not perfect; there were challenges, difficulties, moments of frustration. But the hardships were shared, the burdens were lessened by the strength of the community, the love of Chitra, and the quiet contentment that had become his constant companion. He had found a new beginning, a new life, a new love – a love that was as deep as the earth, as vast as the sky, as enduring as the river that flowed through

the heart of his new home. The city had stripped him bare; the village had clothed him in peace, purpose and the promise of a future he could scarcely have imagined. A future with Chitra, a future brimming with the simple joys of a life lived authentically, a life woven into the rich tapestry of his newfound community. He had found himself, not in the heights of ambition, but in the quiet depths of love and belonging, a love born amidst the paddy fields and nurtured by the gentle rhythms of village life.

Five years had passed since Kumar traded the cacophony of Mumbai for the gentle rhythm of life in Chitra's village. The city, once a symbol of ambition and relentless pursuit, now existed only as a faded photograph in his memory – a stark contrast to the vibrant tapestry of his present life. His once sharp city clothes were replaced by the comfortable simplicity of khadi, his polished shoes exchanged for worn leather sandals. The transformation wasn't just external; it was a deep-seated shift in his very being. The restless energy that had once consumed him had been replaced by a quiet, contented hum.

His days were filled with purpose, a purpose he hadn't found in the boardrooms and skyscrapers of his former life. He continued to work with Chitra's family, his hands still stained with the earth, but now with a practiced ease, a familiarity born of years spent nurturing the land. He had become a vital part of the village, his expertise in urban planning, once deemed irrelevant, now adapted to improve the village infrastructure. He helped design a more efficient irrigation system, earning the deep respect and gratitude of the villagers. His city skills weren't simply a relic of the past but tools for positive change within his new community. The respect he earned wasn't measured in financial success, but in the genuine smiles and heartfelt thanks of those whose lives he touched.

His pottery continued to flourish. His pieces, once simple expressions of rural life, had evolved, incorporating elements of both his city and village aesthetics. He had created a unique style, a fusion of urban precision and rural artistry, earning recognition at regional craft fairs. The small income helped supplement the family's income, and even allowed for small improvements to their home,each upgrade a testament to their shared efforts and growing prosperity. The money wasn't the point though; it was the satisfaction of creating something beautiful, something meaningful, something that reflected the balance he had found within himself.

His relationship with Chitra deepened with each passing year. Their love story, initially a quiet whisper, had blossomed into a vibrant, enduring flame. It wasn't defined by passionate declarations but by the shared burden of daily life, the unspoken understanding that existed between two souls intertwined in the fabric of their community. Their laughter echoed through the village, a testament to their happiness, a rhythm that blended seamlessly with the natural sounds of their home. Their shared life wasn't a fairy tale, but a realistic and beautifully crafted story of two people finding fulfillment in simple joys. They were building a life together, brick by brick, their love as strong as the foundations of their home.

He continued to mentor the village children. He taught them not just arithmetic and reading, but also the value of hard work, respect for their elders, and the importance of community. His classes weren't held in sterile classrooms but under the shade of the banyan tree, the lessons interwoven with tales of his city experiences and his journey to find peace in rural life. He became a bridge between two worlds, teaching them about the vastness of the world beyond their village, yet emphasizing the importance of their roots, their culture, and their deep connection to the land. He had even become something of a mediator, using his understanding of both urban and rural perspectives to help resolve conflicts within the village. His calm demeanor and balanced approach earned him the respect of even the most hardened villagers. His ability to listen, to understand different viewpoints, and to find common ground had made him an indispensable part of the community. His unique skillset was not something to be kept to himself, but rather, something to be shared, to help build bridges and cultivate understanding among his neighbors. His life was a constant cycle of planting, harvesting, creating, teaching, and connecting. It was a life of rhythm and routine, punctuated by the vibrant energy of festivals and the quiet intimacy of evenings spent with Chitra under the starlit sky. He had found a rhythm that suited him perfectly, a tempo that allowed him to appreciate the simple gifts of life. He learned the art of patience, of watching things grow, of understanding the natural ebb and flow of existence, a stark contrast to the relentless pace of city life. He learned the value of human connection, of working together, of sharing both burdens and joys. The experiences had shaped him, matured him, and given him a depth of character that was profoundly enriching. One evening, as the sun dipped below the horizon, painting the sky in hues of orange and gold, Kumar and Chitra sat on their porch, their hands intertwined. The scent of jasmine and freshly cooked rice filled the air. The children played nearby, their laughter mingling with the gentle chirping of crickets. Chitra leaned against him, her head resting on his shoulder. "Do you ever miss the city?" she asked softly, her voice barely audible above the night sounds.

Kumar smiled, a slow, contented smile that reached his eyes. "Sometimes," he admitted, "I miss the convenience, the energy. But I never miss the emptiness." Chitra squeezed his hand. "You found your purpose here, Kumar," she said, her voice filled with love and admiration. "You found your peace." He looked at her, at the serenity reflected in her eyes, at the contentment that radiated from her being. He had found more than peace; he had found belonging, a deep connection to a community, and a love that was as enduring as the land itself. He had found a life filled with purpose, a life that was both meaningful and fulfilling, a life that he would cherish forever. The city had been a chapter in his life, a pivotal one, but this - this was his epilogue, a life he had built with his own hands, a life that was his own beautiful creation. It was a life of quiet joy, of profound connection, and of unwavering love. And that, he realized, was more than he had ever dared to dream of. The city had offered him ambition; the village had offered him a soul. And he wouldn't trade it for anything.

Dear Kumar,

I don't know if I deserve to write to you after everything. I'm not sure if these words will ever reach you, or if you will even want to read them. But still, I write, not to erase what I did, but to finally say what I couldn't back then.

I have played this letter in my head a hundred times. None of the versions feel right. How do you write to someone whose silence has become louder than your presence? How do you speak to someone you hurt when all you ever wanted was to protect them?

What I did, I carry it with me every day. Not as punishment, but as the shadow of what I lost. You were the only person who saw me not as a perfect aspirant or a burdened daughter, but just as Chitra, vulnerable, fierce, confused, soft. You never asked me to prove anything. And I broke that trust, not just with a mistake, but with my silence, with the fear that kept me from being honest when it mattered most.

But Kumar, amid all the guilt, there are still some memories that hold me together, and most of them have you in them.

I still remember the day we studied in the library for hours, and you forgot your own notes because you were too busy explaining my doubts with that quiet patience of yours. How strange that even then, you never looked tired around me.

And that day when we shared chai at the corner stall after your long shift, the rain was falling, our sleeves were soaked, but you still took off your bag and shielded me with it like it was something precious. You didn't say anything. You just smiled. And for a moment, the whole city blurred into the background.

I remember the way you used to write my name in your notebook, hidden in poetry you never shared with anyone. The way you noticed my silence before I did. The way you always said "main hoon na" like it could hold my whole world together.

I think the part that hurts the most is that you were **home**, and I walked away from it.

You never shouted. You never blamed. You stood there like a wall that cracked quietly but never collapsed on me. That stillness hurt more than any words ever could.

Kumar, I want to tell you something, not to ask for you back, not to win your forgiveness, but to offer the truth with the respect it always deserved. **You loved me the way I always wanted to be loved, without condition, without noise, without bargaining. And I failed to love you the same way.**

You were the only man who ever chose me even in my chaos. And even after everything, I believe somewhere deep down, you still hold a place for me , maybe not in your arms, but in your silence. And that is more than I could ask for.

I heard you went back home. I hope your soil heals you. I hope your mornings are quieter now, your nights less heavy. I hope your chai tastes sweet again. And I hope, someday, you fall in love again, not with another person, but with **yourself**, with the boy who came from the village with nothing but books, faith, and a storm in his chest.

And if ever, under a tree, on a winter morning, while the village wakes slowly and your pen moves across a diary page, you think of me, I hope it's without pain. Just a memory. Just softness.

This isn't a letter asking for another chance. It's a folded piece of goodbye, dipped in apology, dried in memory, sealed with hope.

Take care of yourself.

Main tha. Tu thi. Aur kahani reh gayi,

Mohabbat kabhi khatam nahi hoti... bas khamoshi mein likhi jaati hai

Back Matter

From the Author's Heart

"Kuch kahaniyan likhi nahi jaati... woh bas jee li jaati hain."

This story is not just about a boy named Kumar and a girl named Chitra. Yeh kahani un sapno ki hai jo shehron ke raaste mein kahin dhundhla jaate hain. Un khamoshiyon ki hai jo dil ke andar cheekh ban kar ghoomti rehti hain. Aur un rishthon ki hai jinka matlab samajhne ke liye kabhi door jaana padta hai… kabhi laut kar aana padta hai.

When I began writing this novel, I wasn't just telling a story , main apne kuch adhure jazbaat, kuch khoye hue lamhe, aur kuch unkahe sawaalon ko likh raha tha. Kumar ki tarah hum sab ne kabhi na kabhi kisi apne ko piche chhod diya hai... sirf iss umeed mein ki kal kuch aur behtar hoga. Lekin behtar kya hota hai, yeh samajhne mein kabhi kabhi ek poori zindagi lag jaati hai.

Agar aapne kabhi kisi se itna pyaar kiya hai ki usse bhoolna apne aap ko bhoolne jaisa laga ho , Agar aap kabhi kisi gali se guzre ho jahan aapka bachpan rehta tha , Toh shayad yeh kahani aapki bhi hai.

Yeh novel un logon ke liye hai jo khud se kabhi door ho gaye the... Aur unke liye bhi, jo intezaar kar rahe hain kisi ke wapas aane ka.

– Bhirgu Shukla

With all my heart, for all the hearts that ever broke silently.

सरलता से असफलता ...

Love is Abstraction not attraction…

www.ingramcontent.com/pod-product-compliance
Ingram Content Group UK Ltd.
Pitfield, Milton Keynes, MK11 3LW, UK
UKHW041352190726
13845UKWH00026B/563

9 789334 369762